# THE TRAGEDY OF WESLEYAN

## A CHARIOTEER'S SON

"A line you might suppose was wrong,-
He stole from Greek or Latin song."
To my pupils - 1920

Published in India by:

AV Samant

Flat No. B4, Greenwood Meadows,

Candolim 403515

Bardez, Goa



First published 2018

ISBN 978-93-5311-583-8

**DISCLAIMER:**

WRITER    Did you see that? Did you see what they
did?
Did you see what they did to me: that
they
Did wield their sticks above my head and
they
Rent my clothes and beat me all black
and blue;
Until I cried out in pain and "desist,"
"Desist", qouth I, but they did not stop
till
They felt my punishment hath been
given
Unto me. Punishment? And what pray,
was
My crime: That am I writer and I
Have written a story that they doth
claim
Is theirs and that I have stolen and have
Barbarised it, that I so inspired
Was by their tale that I did use it to
Make it mine own and tell my own, and
in
Its course I have changed what was dear
to
Them and have mangled their story line

and
Have represented their characters in
Manner that they did not appreciate?

That is my crime? It hath been said once
that
"The good and great Demophilus hath a
Story writ then by Plautus barbarised"
And if Plautus hath done so, why not I?
For good people, know that we, those
that do
Barbarise, do so not out of hate, but
Out of way too much love for the first
that
It should stay with us, and way too little
Talent for the second that it should not
Stand up to the first, that it should not be
At all that good. Yet, know, kind people,
that
As we work we put a blindfold on our
Eyes that doth take us stumbling through
the long
Narrative, its twisting, turning alleys
To land us aface angered trouble that
Hath sticks in their hands and
punishment on
Their minds; yet it doth happen thus

because
We blindfolded did not see, not because
We meant to insult or to anger ye.

And now, all of ye, others, that doth sit
And seen me beat, that have gathered
here to
See what the fuss was all about, the play,
That did so much ruckus cause, to see if
It hath been created less and barb'rised
More, hear ye and know ye that if it doth
Offend ye as it hath offended them
Think not to chase after me when ye have
Seen the play, to pursue me, and strike
me
For that already transpired, and that
hath
Already been done: I have been chased
and
Beaten up. Know ye, folks, that this
writer
Has been beaten up and he has paid
price
For this audacity that thou art now
Here gathered all together to witness.

And with that I go now to soak and to

Comfort my aches and pains and all my well

Beaten bones in a hot bath while you watch

My work. But here again, know ye that the

Writer has been beaten, folks; the writer

Has been beaten; and sit back yourselves, just

Be entertained, if ye can, just enjoy!

## PEOPLE IN THE PLAY:

### ଓ House of Hector ଓ

◆ Servants: Bill the cook, Tina the maid, Tom the butler.

◆ Scribe: Barobus

◆ Royals of Axainos: Elowyn and Hector.

◆ The Queen's Guard:  Sergei

### ଓ Camp of the Ortellii ଓ

◆ Sons of Ortellius: Anaxarkos, Dion, Anselm

◆ Mentor and Guide: Herakles

◆ Men and Warriors: Ellis, Anius, Malacus, Typhus, Prefect

◆ Old woman in Dubros : Nanna Beth

### ଓ Camp of the Honorii ଓ

◆ Men and Warriors: Abdon the Grandsire, Cyrus the master, Hadrus of Ibrahimya, Fritz

◆ Sons of Honorius: Aristos, Norman

◆ Wesleyan

## Act 1

### CHORUS

But let's leave him, for he hath done his
work
As best he could for being the grouch
and growl
He is, we need him not; so let's proceed
And let us from here away to the land,
The land of Axainos where the weather
Hath there been filled with storms of late
and which
Hath seen continual rain and fallen to
Disrepair since its king hath been
deceased.

Axainos, the land of gold and sea, that
King Ortellius hath ruled well to make its
People with bread and circus satiate;
But now he is dead and his rule hath
passed
On to his son and all, they say, is not
Well in that land that was at one time
rich.

It is not as though Anaxarkos, the
Son of Ortellius would rule less worthy
Than his good father, or would not have

ruled As well; but Anaxarkos, was the
son
Of Elowyn, the queen and only wife
Of Ortellius that did belong to far,
Foreign climes, and that made the new
young king
Only half Axainian, and thus was he
Rejected by half the land's populace.

So upon the old king's death did the
winds
Of strife roll silently into the land,
Which was being covered with the
darkening
Clouds that threatened storms of the
future. No
Sooner did the young heir ascend the
throne
Was he deposed by dissent that was lead
By his cousin, son of Honorius, the
Brother of the deceased king. There did
the
Old king die, and here his nephew
deposed
His son, saying, unlike Anaxarkos
He, Aristos,  was of full Axainian
Blood and more fitting to be ruler than

The dark skinned Anaxarkos. And thus
this
Contention to the new king was by half
The kingdom supported and that did
stall
The transition of power throwing the
land
Into chaos and confusion with no
Settlement in sight when the land into
Factions twain was  divided and the
peace
Gave way to the violence and fear, and
the Land's fruitfulness gave way to death
and dearth.

This unrest and disorder lasted for a
Year when each side fought the other
side with
No resulting solution until the
Distressed folks went up to the elders of
The land, silently watching their state in
Deterioration, and the elders were
Implored by the people to intervene.
The drawing of lots was the solution
That the elders did put forward that
would
Inform them of what the Gods did desire,

And whom the Gods thought best to rule
the land.

Queen Elowyn, Anaxarkos' mother,
Had been against this, some thought
rightly so,
For well known was the thieving nature
of
Aristos, which made the act of drawing
Lots suspect in his hands, but then
rightly
Or wrongly she agreed and lots were
drawn
To fall in favour not of her three sons,
But in the favour of Honorius' sons;
And thus the throne of Axainos was
deemed
To pass from the clan of good Ortellius'
Unto the clan of the rude Honorius.

Aristos had exulted upon the
Draw: 'The throne and crown belonged
to him now'
He hath cried, but Anaxarkos and his
Supporters refused to accept this draw,
And they did protest in one voice, to say
That had the lots been fairly drawn, and

had
The dice not been loaded, the Gods
would have
Spoken for them; they declared Aristos
To be a crook and thief, and reaffirmed
The right of Anaxarkos to the rule.

Thus was there to the détente solution
None, but manifestation new that did
Generate more unrest and violence
Throughout the land; when the people to
the
Elders turned again that then suggested
A year's exile for Anaxarkos and
His men the while which Aristos would
rule
The Kingdom, and when the exile was
done
A battle would be fought to decide
which
Faction would be rulers. Anaxarkos'
Mother Elowyn had thought against this
Resolution as well, but again had
She silenced her doubts to say that
Elders
To her husband's rule had been advisors
And thus they must have in their

decision,
Retained the good of Axainos in mind,
And so it  happened thus that the sons of
Ortellius went on a year long exile.

The days did roll and the time did pass
which
The sons of Ortellius in exile spent
And sons of Honorius in palaces
Lived, but in the near court of justice did
The God of fate present himself again
To the matter solve; and that was at
where
Axainos now stood, at the cusp of war,
When with exile done, sons of Ortellius
Themselves stationed at Dubros, from
where they
Sent their friend and mentor Herakles to
Speak with the elders and to demand
their
Wealth be returned or prepare
themselves to
Face the battle and their termination.
The foremost thought of Herakles as he
Rode on to Axainos was that the son
Of Ortellius, a man of peace, had asked
Him to negotiate with the knowledge

that
Should the battle be the result of this
Meeting, it would leave a devastation
Its wake, and therefore had he asked him
to
First try to negotiate a partition
Of the land to enable subsistence,
And had asked him to try avoid a war.

The darkening clouds of impending
doom did
Gather in the skies and the strong winds
did
Blow when Herakles to his homeland
rode
Amidst the testimonials of the men
That the omens did not bode too well
and
That the rivers had been flowing
upstream
Seen, and waters witnessed spewing out
of
Wells, and bloody rain falling from the
skies
At early morn had been observed by all.

The unwelcome city gates were reached,

and
Herakles who knew that Aristos was
Not one to go halves on anything, and
Feared that now when the Kingdom was
his,
It would be not relinquished without a
Fight. Herakles entered the city and
On the ruined marble font placed his
foot,
And 'bout him saw the city's people
strained,
And the citizens scared of what was to
Befall them in the near future. With the
Thought in Herakles' mind that all he
could
Do was try his best for the populace,
And the sons of Ortellius, he walked
with
Quick and detemined steps up to the
Hall
Of the council, where was arranged by
the
Elders, a council for peace that would
aim
To decide this unfortunate land's fate
That seemed to firmly, irrevocably
Stand aface the opening jaws of war.

## Act 1, Scene 1

**House of Hector, Axainos**

**(The servants Bill, Tom and Tina come in.)**

BILL        Tom and Tina, but do listen, and hear
            My tale of woe, and of my dream last
            night when
            I saw myself diced and all my bones
            ground, Then mixed in almond's milk
            and amidon,
            And added sifted cloves of gillyflowers
            And then with cinnamon, wine, ginger
            was spiced,
            And white sugar was added to cut heat,
            And in beurre noisette roasted till fine
            browned;
            Thus baked was I then plated and served
            up
            To hungry, ruthless men that in the field
            Did sup upon the tried and toasted Bill,
            I, Bill the baker's son, but girl, talk to me.

TINA        Move thy carcass. There is work to be
            done.

BILL        But we, are just servants and quite
            useless,
            In Lord Hector's house where we are
            quite so

Indispensable and so needed there
To feed and clean, and cover up, but we
Will not be sent to war, will we, will we?
I am a baker small with knowledge none
Of wielding weapons, that useth his hands
Just to knead bread and to stir soups, but speak.

TOM     Thinks I that thou art just as good as what
They need for thou wouldst add to piles of dead
Bodies just as well as any soldier
Would, and fill the field when killed as well as
Any strong and beefy army man would.

BILL    But, Tommy, tell me do, dear Tom, thou art
Butler; if thou and Tina here, a maid
Wilst not be made to go fight then why
Will I, Billy the cook, be singled out,
With lime and parsley stuffed, basted like a
Turkey to be then packed of to the war?

TINA    I know not about thee, but Tina here
Will not be called to fight as though a

cock
Tossed into the market brawl with
feathers
Flying, and no one, I mean no one, can
Send the beautiful goddess to her death.

BILL        Well, I do swear upon my cauliflower
Roast and pecan nuts, but who could
want to
Send me, epitome of piety,
To death as if I hailed the goddess not?

TINA        She, the ghoul, the owl, the vulture,
mother
Of the enemy for whom we slave day
In and out, come here do that, fetch this,
will
Kill us with the working first and then
send
Us to war to kill us over like a
Twice done pig upon the spit, but, mark
thou
These my words, Bill Cat, if we are ever
Called to the fight, the Lady Elowyn
Will be the one signing on the order.

BILL        Not she, sayest thou, but softly speak,
wilt
Thou not for she be, but beyond these

walls
From whence perchance doth hear us as
we speak?

TINA    Let her hear, and what care I that these
walls
That hold her, she owns not, and she is
but
A guest in mine Lord Hector's
household, whose I
A servant be, and not hers, not never
hers,
And get this straight Bill, e'en if us,
women
Are not sent afield to fight, better than
Men fare we, right here, at home, and I
am
Yet even begun to fight the mother
Of the enemy, so whining baker
Hist and watch thou mine deadly arms
and keep
Thine eyes on mine silent, but deathly
knocks.

TOM    Look busy for master comes this way
Unto the house with the Lord Herakles.
(Enter Hector and Herakles.)

HECTOR  Go thou and convey to the lady that

    Lord Herakles requests to meet with her.

HERAKLES And how is she our sister much
    maligned?

HECTOR   Well,  what can I say, that the demands of
    This past year hath changed her; since her boys left
    She reduced her speech in witness mute to
    Silently watch what transpired in her land:
    The reason I can tell thee not, but she
    Doth speak much less, and worry more and tired
    Seems than did earlier, which makes me wonder
    If she would have more contented been hath she
    Taken away by her sons on exile.

HERAKLES  This past year was way too arduous and the
    Strain was carried easily not even
    By the men; though here she may have suffered
    Much, thanks to you, she has been kept alive.

(Enter Elowyn)

ELOWYN  Loving brother, Herakles, how art thou.

HERAKLES Warmest greetings, I bring thee from
            Dubros,
            M'lady from all those there that loveth
            thee.

HECTOR  And here your happiness shared I will
            leave
            The two of you to converse and for the
            Palace leave where the work doth awaits
            me.
            (Hector exits)

ELOWYN And so Herakles, pray tell me, have the
            Esteemed members of the council set
            right
            The Heaven and the earth again with
            trees
            And rivers and the skies put back in
            Places proper as their esteemed nature
            Hathe deemed for their services past
            rendered?

HERAKLES The council ended early and it failed.

ELOWYN  But, who was fooled by the
            announcement of
            Its intent, as shows of purpose go which

Are to drive the masses's opinion and
For their outcomes to be disccused in
fairs
And squares;  since that was done, its
purpose was
Achieved  and althought it was a failure,
Yet again it was not so for was the
Status quo not maintained for seventh
Time, the seventh different way possible?
Yes, of course, it was and thus the council
Meeting though failed could not be
termed as such.
Please, tell me of this successful failure.

HERAKLES Well, it happened so, my lady, that
         though
         Being well reasoned with and spoken to,
         the
         Son, Aristos, refused to accept each
         And every resolution possible;
         Nay, he did not so solutions refuse
         As much refused to listen to a thing
         That was contrary to his own point of
         View, which then brought forth much
         raving, and much
         Ranting and emotions on all sides, and
         Nothing, just nothing much achieved at
         all,

To be then finally told by me that they
Should keep the throne, and to his
cousins give
A share as subsistance, to which he said
That not even enough land as can be
Touched by a needles' tip would be let
go.
Thus was there nothing more left be said.

ELOWYN  And then, the council endeth there, did
it?

HERAKLES It would have earlier endedeth, but for
That villain, Wesleyan that kept it on
The boil by strutting up and down quite
full
Of his importance' air, unearthing all
Grievances past, and filling his belov'd
King, as he kept calling Aristos, with
Remembrance of his greatness, and at the
Same ensuring he made the sirs irate.

ELOWYN  And now do pause a while there,
Herakles,
For thou hast just now spoken of the one
Whom I did wish to talk to thee about,
And therefore let us leave aside the sirs
That nothing but more trouble further
bring.

HERAKLES Honestly, sister, I do think that were
           It not for his friend, Honorius' son who's
           Not otherwise that unreasonable,
           Would be easier spoken to and reasoned.

ELOWYN  What dost thou think then of the
           proposal
           To take him to one side and speak to
           him.

HERAKLES Does my lady refer to Aristos
           Or the other?

ELOWYN                You know.

HERAKLES                            The lady jests?

ELOWYN  Those less tired and less hapless in their
           Lives do jest, Herakles; every single
           Of my words are now the sounds of
           drying
           Greens that are filled with the brown and
           aging
           Earnestness that crackles with its years
           for
           It carries not the youthful sap of hope
           Lost to it, and those in such a state have
           Neither time nor luxury to jest , and
           Though they maybe in vain and
           hopeless, their

Words are never uttered in mockery.

HERAKLES But, pardon me, m'lady that I ask thee
Again if she wisheth me to speak to
The charioteer's son; have I heard that
right?

ELOWYN More now, the face and strength of
Aristos
Than he is aught less, but do take him to
The side; tell him that he should Aristos
Leave, instead join us, join Anaxarkos
For Wesleyan, though not one of us, is
One of us, in ideals, would be safe to
Say, but if he does come o'er to our side,
Will my Anaxarkos, though my eldest,
Make Wesleyan, the king of Axainos.

HERAKLES You know my lady, he may not agree.

ELOWYN And yet, we do not err when we do try.
Try we must, though he may return us
with
Heads bowed down in shame of being
refused, we
Stand no worse off than before, but if by
Some wild stroke of luck he does agree,
then
We will avoid war, and still the throne of
Axainos retain; do thou that I ask.

HERAKLES I would do better if I better knew
　　　　　What to say to him.

ELOWYN　　　　　　　　　　　Tell him that he
　　　　　is
　　　　　Duty bound to be with us, to cease this
　　　　　Fighting against us.

HERAKLES　　　　　　　　　　He will not
　　　　　listen
　　　　　And needs must that I reason with this
　　　　　man?

ELOWYN　Tell him that he is not one of them, and
　　　　　That if with us, he will be made the king.

HERAKLES But, thou speakest as though thou dost
　　　　　not know
　　　　　And thou know'st full well that he
　　　　　desires
　　　　　Not the throne of Axainos for himself,
　　　　　But to kill thy sons is what he wants, to
　　　　　Ensure the enthronement of Aristos.

ELOWYN　And yet, the strength of Aristos in the
　　　　　Battlefield is nothing but the strength of
　　　　　Wesleyan, and separate that one man
　　　　　From the fray, and you have Aristos, and
　　　　　Nay his brothers, and his entire army
　　　　　Totally defenseless on the field, and

          Wilt thou try speak to him is all I ask?

HERAKLES  I will try my lady, for thy sake, but
          I wish to know thy thoughts about thy
          sons
          At Dubros and if this strange meeting
          with
          Wesleyan is to be ta'en back to them?

ELOWYN  Say nothing to my sons at all about
          Should we be sent ashame and made to
          fail;
          Just tell them that all ways of achieving
          Peace hath failed, therefore Anaxarkos
          Hath no option left, but prepare for war.

HERAKLES It hath been writ in the scriptures of
          yore
          That if a task is to be accomplished
          And if one doth wish to petition the
          Spirits of success then the best place for
          It to be is by the water's side and
          So before to Dubros I depart from
          Hence I will attempt beside the Pontus
          To entreat the perchance softer, and the
          Maternal Wesleyan, if there be one,
          And we will see how it does transpire.
          Hector told me that thou dost make
          attempts

For to engage a scribe and in that thou
Art not succeeding and art not allowed.

ELOWYN When he burned the records of the
kingdom
Past I watched on enraged, yet Herakles,
With the enfeebled tries of one that hath
No power to do the thing that's right in
the
Governance of one who to thy right is
Wrong, this past entire year my single
task
Hath been to find a scribe and rewrite
that
Hath been destroyed. Of course, as one in
war
Of attempts aface storms of tyrrany
Hath all this year my efforts borne no
fruit,
Whereat have I been termed a raving, old
Woman that nothing does, but attempts
one
Man after the next to put the paper
To his pen.

HERAKLES                             After thy sons left did
they
Burn the records?

ELOWYN      And with them the proof of
      Our existence, and therefore, needs be that
      We must ourselves, our existence restore,
      And leave we things as they are now, all of
      History will leave be ignorant of
      Us, and all the while the princeling that doth
      Occupy my husband's seat will put his
      Father where did sit the father of my
      Son, but then the skies above doth darken
      Every passing day and auger that the
      Gods with Aristos' rule remain not pleased
      And there shall be witnessed Kingship's change e'en
      If we do pay the most horrendous price.

HERAKLES If Gods want war, my lady, then, who are
      We otherwise decree, and all attempts
      To achieve otherwise will of their own
      Their failure meet and then will we enforced
      Be to accept that out of ego's pride
      We refused to adhere to the word, but,

My lady allow me to take thy leave.

ELOWYN  For thy help and for thy understanding
Dear Herakles I do thee thank; God speed,
My brother; fare thee well and God speed.

## Act 1 Scene 2

**Palace courtyard, Dubros**

NANNA BETH Anaxarkos! Where art thou and hear my
    Plea for I stand here in expectation of
    An audience, and I, a lady of
    A hundred years that knew thy father, and
    His father even, and then thee, before
    Thou wast deposed; so, young Anaxarkos,
    Forget not that thou art protector of
    The weak and the aged, and give thou thy
    Errant  audience to this woman old; so
    Anaxarkos, present thyself to me.

PREFECT Here, you, cease this shouting at once, away.

NANNA BETH  No, you, but listen to me, boy, and tell
    Me whether this the palace is, the one
    In the market place they say is where the
    Ortellius's sons reside in secrecy
    At Dubros here; if this be that then will
    Anaxarkos give an audience to me.

PREFECT Whyfore, old lady, dost thou wish to

know?

NANNA BETH  Leave me then, you pup the upstart of the
Regime new knowest not to bend before
The wise that doth appear not so wise, and
Anaxarkos, if thou art within, do
Hear my words and show thy face to this sad
Lady seer of what thou cans't see not and
Doth wish to know if thou wise and caring
Art as thy ancestors before, my child,
Do present thyself to one who be eaons
More aged than thou art.

PREFECT　　　　　　　　　Cease this shouting.

NANNA BETH No, leave me, go about your duty, you
Young weasel, go, off.

PREFECT　　　　　　　　Must I throw thee out?

NANNA BETH Leave me, Anaxarkos, Anaxarkos.
(Enter Anaxarkos)

ANAXARKOS What is this noise?

PREFECT　　　　　　　　Lord Anaxarkos, I
Will instantly have her removed from

hence.

ANAXARKOS Is she not Nanna Beth of whom I
        have
        Been told by people of Dubros; unhand
        Her then, and ask her what she wants of
        me.

NANNA BETH  My son, I ask thee for a favour; say
        Not no to me!

ANAXARKOS         Soldier, bring her here; speak.

NANNA BETH Kindly prince art thou, dear
        Anaxarkos,
        Honest and just as afore thy fathers
        Were; all Axainos doth praise the eldest
        Son of Elowyn as just and honest.

ANAXARKOS  Were it that simple, Beldam and was
        the
        Line between the good and evil even
        Now as clear as it was when the winds
        were
        Not muddied by the war's approach and
        the
        Dust of chaos and confusion enraged
        To obfuscate the clarity of minds,
        But in the midst of all this, dear Nanna,
        I see an anxiety wrinkled on thy

Brow a face so ancient that it perchance
Hath seen all that it canst seen, and thus
for
Antiquity to be worried in such
A manner bodes not well for those of us
In charge, and therefore with the hope
that thy
Enchanneled words will serve us as a
guide,
Make thou thy mind all free from fear
and speak.

NANNA BETH Anaxarkos, I am old and stupid.
A grandson, all of thirteen years of age,
Have I, named Ellis, who is mine only
Support that hath been called for war,
and who,
Undoubtedly being tender in his years
Will perish in this battle, and then with
Him gone who have I as sustainance;
So please, Lord Anaxarkos, give me back
My grandson.

ANAXARKOS                    Where is her boy?

PREFECT                                      Facing
the
Training in the camps, my Lord, and
cared for.

ANAXARKOS Bring him here to see me, and
                    meanwhile, this
                    Woman take within to be looked after.

NANNA BETH Wait, but no, but wait, do wait; there
                    is more;
                    My lord, I have much more to tell to thee.

PREFECT   Be quiet, old and ugly witch, but this
                    One here, my Lord, known a menace in
                    the
                    Market place, should not be emboldened
                    for
                    Once she doth start speaking, she does
                    not know
                    How to cease and wanders whence the
                    normal
                    Would avoid to go.

ANAXARKOS                       Let me hear her, still.

NANNA BETH Thou art  good my lad, Prince
                    Anaxarkos
                    And in manner of thy ancestors a
                    Worthy son, and yet, my boy, despite
                    that,
                    Must I ask thee to be warned by visions
                    That I see, but yet I see my visions,
                    That do portend that thou soon wilt kill.

PREFECT   My lord, she now thee insulteth, but please
Command thou me to have her ta'en way.

NANNA BETH No, no, but wait, and leave me, listen to
Me, thou a juvenal attempting to
Be a king: I see the distant future
That appeareth near here, and in it I
See what, bodies dead, and killed by thee, and
Plundered, mutilated, lying in the
Seas of blood and in their midst I see thou
Red and bloodied also art and searching.
Thou the murdered searchest; for whom is it
That thou searchest: be not thine enemy,
But no, thy brother searchest thou, there he
Is found lying dead somewhere and killedeth by
Wesleyan, is it, no, by Wesleyan
Thy brother's not killed, but thee, by thee.

PREFECT   Better watch thy words, I warn you.

NANNA BETH  Yes, Anaxarkos I lie not to you
                That I see is a brother killdeth dead
                Beside thy hand, with thy brother
                bloodied
                Sword; there I see he lieth dead beside
                Thy cruel foot toucheth his inertness.

ANAXARKOS Which brother?

NANNA BETH                    And here, Anaxarkos
                give
                To me thine hands thy strong and kindly
                hands
                And yes, I know the powers fool me not
                For on thy palm as if on the page of
                "Anaxarkana", see I that word, that
                Dying word thy brother spoke of last as
                Plea for life and it doth read, quite plain
                and
                Simple, yet quite deathly in urgency
                And an "aitch" is on thy palm beside an
                "ee"
                An "el" and endeth with a "pee" that's
                "help".

PREFECT  I beseech my lord to take her words not
                Serious; and she will now begin to wail.

NANNA BETH Hear ye people all that he hath killed
                his

Brother, people, like a dog hath he struck
Him heartless dead and now doth look
for his
Remains, and finds them not, and shame
on him,
The shame and more the shame of it - the
shame,
The shame, the shame, the shame, the
shame and more.

PREFECT  But cease this senseless lamentation and
Yet she will now beat her head, and is
not
Quite right of mind, my lord; command
thou
To have her put her away.

ANAXARKOS                                    To the kitchens,
Take her to have her taken care of with
Respect, dragoon, as though the ages
thou
Wouldst respect;  have my guardsman's
imprudence
Not have me face the wrath of history;
My good aunt fear not for thy grandson's
life.
(Enters Dion)

NANNA BETH Thou wilst kill a brother, Anaxarkos

Forget not thine own brother thou wilst
kill.

(Exit prefect and Nanna Beth)

DION    With which ne'er do well dost thou
pratest now?

ANAXARKOS A woman old whose grandson is to
be
Released, and yes, I see that from my
words
Thou turnest in exasperation and
Thou now undoubtedly wilst berate me;
But even so the boy doth needs release.

DION    A hundred thousand soldiers to us by
Arcadia sent hath been by thee till now
Released and now you tell me that some
more
Are to be given up, or could it be,
Dear brother, that prepareth we not for
The battle of our lives, but only the
Festivities which can or cannot be
Attended to by all if it be not
Convenient; shall I save us all the
Trouble and let go the entire army?

ANAXARKOS The boy that seeks to be released is
yet
To be a man, and Arcadia's soldiers

            Are but farmers with their pitchforks
            wrenched 'way
            And pikes enthrusted unto them with
            which
            Were they expected to make war with
            best
            Trained military of the enemy?

DION      I will not argue with thee, brother, but
            Will say our army is too weak in that
            Our size is way too small compared to
            theirs
            For which the strength of numbers,
            trained,
            Untrained
            Is now the need and if we send each one
            Away we will be left will but a small
            Band of well trained men which to my
            mind is
            Less effective than a force that shews the
            Higher, and therefore the better number.

ANAXARKOS Number Dion, number, is the man to
            thee
            Naught but number or is he a person
            And possessor of a heart which be the
            Insurance of families and with one
            Person thou dost kill not none but ten,

and

While I understand that we are at a

War, let us not turn a man into a

Number yet, my man, not yet, but wait a

While before we all inevitably

Do become the monsters undoubtedly

That we will as the days proceed into

war.

(Enter Anselm)

DION          Anselm, brother, have we some more of

news?

ANSELM   The message that hath come reporting

safe

Herakles at Axainos hath none to

Follow suit, but we do still await some.

ANAXARKOS With it will Herakles certainly bring

Peace I know, or yet in case the council

Fails, which may well do, our mother

will step

Forth to attempt some kind of settlement,

Of that I certain am as well for how

Can she expect us to our elders fight,

Who naught but are our selves reborn

that were

Once born before and then are born

again as

Us to make it such our sire and our
Teacher are the previous two of us three.

DION      Our grandsire and our teacher are not us
And much less are they for us and the
more
Are they faithful dogs to them that hold
firm
The kingdom's throne; to us the sires are
but
A nuisance that doth make all matters
worse,
But look not in anger, Anaxarkos,
That I do address them thus for when I
Aim mine arrow on his face he will not
Be my grandsire, but a dog, the target
To mine orphaned and vengeful
munitions.

ANAXARKOS And that, my dear brother Dion, is as
I
Will have thee know the very reason that,
This war must not take place for no good
will
Out of it come, if its grand result doth
Necessitate grandsire fighting grandson
And a student fighting teacher; and a
Cousin fighting cousin; now dost thou

see?

DION      All I can see is the wench that holds the
Scales askew; and when she beckons me must
The man fight the man, and that remains the
Length, and breadth and extent of thought for me,
Which if too deep doth  leave me out of breath:
No room nor energy to act towards the
Balance nor to set right side up one more.

ANSELM  Here I break in to ask of Wesleyan
But who or what is he to anyone
If not the espouser of threat to us?

DION      That despite being foreign to the problem,
He does his friendly cause take on him to
His enemies annihilate. Worst, the worst
Is he, danger at best, adversary
Formidable that doth shout out be done
In, out with every worthless, excess word
He speaks to undermine his birth from wheels
With which will he each one of us drag to
The destiny of death; and here will e'en

    Anaxarkos own up to the lack of

    Ground to eke out peace with one who

    means but

    Destruction to us, and whom I hate most.

ANAXARKOS While Dion, it maybe true that I too

    Have nothing good to say of Wesleyan,

    Except that if mere hatred be the only

    Word to say of one then better be for

    One that soldiers to his counsel keep for

    Passion doth dispense one's energy in

    Measure worse thought, yes, what have

    ye here?

    (Enter prefect)

PREFECT  A message from Lord Herakles.

ANSELM             What

    hath?

PREFECT  Only word that peace hath failed the

    council.

DION    Call back dispersed farmers of Arcadia.

ANAXARKOS No, Dion wait until Herakles'

    returns,

    When he shall take us to us our mother's

    thoughts

    To tell us if this battle asks for war,

    Or some concession made, or even the

Complete sacrifice, and so rush thou
nothing
Yet, but let things remain for Herakles.
(Anaxarkos leaves)

DION        But, Good Gods, that they bestow dear
            patience
            On us; now, Anselm how on earth are we
            to
            Keep his sensless word; must we
            disobey?

ANSELM      He, our leader dothe lead us to higher
            Forms of existence which may just take
            us
            To the depths of frustration. I know not
            How to talk to him, but to leave him to
            Herakles that hath the patience we have
            Not, but we must continue with our
            work:
            Call the commanders, and brief the
            soldiers
            And get them all to move. Move onward,
            all
            Of us for work hath been thus far long
            stalled.

DION        What about the soldiers of Arcadia?

ANSELM      Yes, they are by us needed and although

Our brother hath commanded their
return,
His ruling will be stayed by my
command
Allowed to me these times and so inform
Them that their release has been
overruled.
(They exit)

========

## Act 1 Scene 3
### The Royal palace, Axainos.

ARISTOS    Wesleyan, where hast thou been my
         man, when
         All requirements asked for thee I had to
         Tell them that the sun art thou that now
         shines
         Us with thy compassion then disappears
         To the other half more battel-worthy.

WESLEYAN But my dear lord, my King, my master,
         and
         Preceptor mine, of Axainos' thou art
         The king and I am, underling, mere son
         Of wheels that can but take the shape of
         that
         Celestial orb not once but seven times,
         Yet canst not match its brilliance once,
         and
         Remains forever mired in the mud
         And rooted to the ground on which thou,
         the
         Sun, thy sandals placest; and as is my
         Job, I've been hard at work for thee, my
         friend,
         My lord, to prove that I remain not friend
         But servant to thy cause, and much better

To one I was at was that clock today,
A wretched time it was that paled a-front
The future when thy soldier, I, infant
Wicker's occupant by thee thy kingdom's
Chancellor made, was made to prove my
friendship's
Worth; e'en then in this war I did remain
For thy protection and to ensure thy
Win and yet still be forever small and
Lowly born forever at thy knees, a
Wesleyan, of thy heart, for thy service.

ARISTOS   And what was it, my friend, that at the
clock
Occurred hath caused thee to be effusive
So early in the morn, and hath made thee
To compete with the croaking of the
frogs
Announcing death of one and arrival
Of the next hour. And though our thanks
are due
Towards thy verbal kisses, less in need
Are we of wordy caresses, my man
And more of striking action as it's war
That we prepareth for, not the national
Theatre. Instead of laying sentences
We now need the laying of the roads that
Will take us to the fight and to our right.

WESLEYAN The roads are completed and the city
　　　　　Hath been to the battle joined for quite some
　　　　　Time now for we did not cut ourselves from
　　　　　Duty to perjure ourself to thee, but
　　　　　Did our reverences and thence hither
　　　　　Came to have our love denied and promise
　　　　　Heartlessly by you called a barratry.

ARISTOS　The roads were consummated by thee,
　　　　　when?

WESLEYAN Before the King can ask Wesleyan for
　　　　　Some thing, it is already done for when
　　　　　Thou by the council wast kept uselessly
　　　　　Engaged, the roads were done and now await
　　　　　Thy inspecting foot walk on them, my
　　　　　leige.

ARISTOS　My friend, thy well excepted love is by
　　　　　Us well accepted, but the one that won't
　　　　　Be left out of prosaic dialogue , yes him
　　　　　Again, our grandsire that hath spoken yet
　　　　　To us the same till now a hundredth time
　　　　　Hath asked of us, to speak of it once

    more
    And so will be here presently and needs
    Must that we tolerate and him receive,
    But first, there is a thing of which I
    wished
    To talk to thee about, for fear of war
    Afore the war, I had till now side
    stepped.

WESLEYAN But anything for you, your majesty.

ARISTOS  Before their man to Dubros hath
    returned,
    What heard I was that he brought thee to
    one
    Side to speak to thee?

WESLEYAN       Did, my lord.

ARISTOS        Saying what?

WESLEYAN To leave Aristos' side, but by the
    wealth
    Of all the world canst thou believe he
    asked
    Me to abandon thee and come on to
    Their side to falsely be Ortellius son;
    Said he, which if I did then I would be
    made
    Axainos' king and would this war be

then
Circumvented whereto my reply was
That my life's aim never was to be the
King, but to remain a servant to mine
And to slay Ariman's to my master,
Which coincidently are those
aforementioned
Sons of Ortellius whom thou expects me
To join, and to destroy whom will I be
True, and those whom I will kill one by
one.
And here,  I ask of you my liege, are they
That green that they did think to ask me
this?

ARISTOS   What did he say when you his crack
refused ?

WESLEYAN Said he not a thing, and walked he
away
But not before I saw his colour change,
Saw him scared, but Aristos, we now
know
How scared they are of me and terrified
Of my ability whereof they will
Be brought down to the deadly dust to be
Uncompassionately leveled to the
ground

       With one attested thrusting of my sword.

ARISTOS  Well, now, that do I find thee newly
       loved
       By Princes of the Dark, I think, better
       Sense wouldst have been for me in
       contentious
       Abdon's stead had I made thee
       Commander.

WESLEYAN By my fate, thou madest me the merest
       Son of wheelers put shine of wealth upon
       My restless badge, but Aristos, never
       My allegiance doubt whereof I owe to
       Ye not as cash for kindness and for your
       Friendship that thou hast on me
       bestowed, for
       That love is not the sort renders
       payment,
       But I owe it to ye as my love for
       You, and for the rest of your
       bestowments
       I remain forever in your debt and
       Forever at your service, forever
       Lowly leveled, and now here they arrive,
       The grand old elders of our fledgeling
       land.
       Good day, twenty more to ye, good

Grandsires.
What would you have us tell your
ancient ears?

ABDON    My ancient ears hath a million times 'fore
heard
The forsworn words that thou hast
spoken just
To my nephew, and my ancient eyes
h'seen
A thousand times the fateful end that
such
Bring. Yet, Cyprus didst thou hear his
worthless
Blather? And, Wesleyan, if thou art the
Truly friend of Aristos  then do him
Good, thou useless man, instead
concealest
His fateful end with words of colour and
With flowers misleading him to wrongly
fight
This war and ultimately annihilate
And bring to end the clan of  Honorius.

WESLEYAN Thy unkind words, Lord Abdon hath
been by
Me heard, that with my kindly silence
shall

Be replied, for if one's wordiness hath
Colour then silence is not colourless
Which when indulged in, doth not
louder shout
Than words, not pierce the less than
dialogue does,
So my silence will thy insults answer.

ABDON        Aristos! As aged men, remainders
Of kingdom's glorious past Cyprus and I
Ask of you, one more, a final time:
Return the throne its rightful owner
And place the son under his father's
crown.

ARISTOS      Grandsire Abdon, thy memory of the
Ages is and it faileth thee as does
Thy mathematics when thou countest not
The numerous times that thou hast asked
it of
Us and then yet as though
inconsequential
Was our speech, and in between we
perchance
Have changeth our mind; so must I
repeat
Again "We will not part with as much
land

Thy little finger covers or thy toe".

WESLEYAN "Nine hundred and ninety-nineth time
succeed
We shall when the nine hundred, ninety
eighth
Hath failed us as does our mathematics.
Grand, old toad counteth beyond fingers
ten.

CYPRUS    Wesleyan, let him speak with his father.

ABDON    Aristos, question is yet unanswered.

WESLEYAN Look thou here old man, this is thy well
worn
Question, and to thine unseeing ancient
Eyes was this, reply offered so many
Times before that at its edges it hath
Now been frayed by our easy overuse.

ABDON    Thou keepest out of this, thou lowborn
scum
That in the gutter of the bitch was born.

ARISTOS   No, Wesleyan don't.

WESLEYAN                          Aristos, restrain
Me not, and know thou Abdon in battle
I can despite my birth bear down upon
All those that you consider to be high
With skills unsurpassed and unbiased

that
Give 'dmission to the low to disembowel
Stomachs of the sons of Ortellius and
Throw their entrails in thy face if only
So that thou canst know who is he born
high
And who is born so blindingly low that
No further than this sad level can he.

ABDON   The thing you threaten to do unto them,
They will unto thee for though thou
thinkest
Thyself to be superior, but know that
Thou art only so in speech not in deed,
And whenst will come the time to show
thy worth
Wilst thou then leave us stranded and to
see
That they are to this battle born not thee.

WESLEYAN You want action, Aba? Well then see
what
I will act upon right now to show thee
What is needed to succeed, birth or berth:
While the first is bestowed quite free of
cost
The second is but by fealty achieved.
And so watch thou, what I will do right

now,
When this considered decision I take
That till this old and open mouth lies not
In deathly silence and eternal gape
And till the echo of his diatribe
Spills not from his lifeless, unmoving
mouth,
I will sit out this war's activities,
I will abstain from the fight.

ARISTOS                                        Wesleyan!

WESLEYAN No Aristos, he's old; therefore, useless
Like a tree diseased that's browned and
withered
And will the battle last a day; no more.
When only for a single day will be
The strength of his beleaguered
weaponry.
When he discarded and unneeded lies
To needs be bidden farewell to will I
Pick up the tip, by entering the fray;
And therefore let the castle born begin
Sans me his dithering ability,
To match action to his chironomy.
(Wesleyan walks out)

ABDON    Observe the haughty, infirm man in
whom

Thou thy trust entire and thy love hast
put.
Observe how he has his infirmness
shown,
And hath in a miser's cowardly way
Before this war hath been decided or
E'en before this war hath been brought
afield
Or 'fore thou hast prepared thine arms,
observe
He hath his support rent, deserted thee.

ARISTOS　Grandsire no, what I observe dismayed is
How elders: my sire, here, that does not
think,
And there, the mother of our enemy
That thinks too much, both attempt to
make breach
'Tween Wesleyan and me, the two of us
Doth try separate. My grandsire, my case
Is not fidelity of Wesleyan,
But my problem is what firmly sits 'side
The enemy: that is thy allegiance

CYPRUS　No, Aristos, not with the enemy,
Nor with ye, but with the Axainian'
throne:
The allegiance of Lord Abdon and I,

Of Cyprus, and also Leroy, my son,
Doth sit with whosoever sits upon
The kingdom's throne, the throne of
Axainos

ARISTOS    Yes, Master Cyprus, therein the differ'nce
Doth lie, wherein all you hath allegiance
To the throne of the kingdom, Wesleyan
Hath allegiance to me and he will fight
For me, and only me, and not for naught
But me, not for the throne, nor for glory,
Not for fame, but for me, me, Aristos.

ABDON    Cyprus, then let this pass, for this is all
We could have done to achieve what had
hoped.
The result is now to be left to Fates,
But hear thou this one final warning, son,
Prince Aristos, that I will leave thee with
And know thou that thy downfall will be
caused
By none other than the very person
Whom thou hath thy entire trust
entrusted.

ARISTOS    I hear thy words, sir, but they scare me
not.

## Act 1 Scene 4
### House of Hector, Axainos.

TINA
It was this very morning,when the sun was shining and the birds were gay and it was promising to be such a happy day, I heard the Lady mention, in the morning room, that the numbers of soldiers in Anaxarkos' army fell short and that if they did not recruit they would not win, and here I would have thee know, Bill, that she said they are wanting for soldiers.

BILL
But, that cannot be, that they could send me to war for look at me: I am so thin and so small.

TINA
She is a horrible woman and in need of someone like me to stab her in the back, and I will have ye know, Billy boy, that I have already begun working towards noble aim of redeeming this good, hardworking, and beautiful world of a rude, contentious, and a proud woman.

(Enter Barobus)

TOM
Tina, is that the man you met in the tavern?

TINA        Of course, I knew he would come back to
            me with his tail in between his legs, and
            what do they call ye this morning sir, be
            it, and what was that name again I forgot
            for the breeze of the morning's sun doth
            erase the dust of night's memory:
            Barobus. I am sure that I heard them call
            thee, Barobus.

BAROBUS  They say that it is my name.

TINA        At the tavern, where we were met when
            in the dim lights of our impoverished
            night I made thee a promise under the
            large lamps when you asked and I
            agreed to let you into the house of Hector
            like you wanted, and now that it is done,
            what else might I allow thee, the one who
            thy majesty is not?

BAROBUS  If you could take me to meet the mother
            of the enemy, and I see the lack of
            interest on your lips, but perhaps if there
            was money in it, but no not just money, a
            lot of money, because money is the
            problem and I could make you, nay all of
            you, you all very rich if you take me to
            see the woman for, you see, I have
            something on her, some information,

wherewith I can stop the battle.

BILL  O, for all the goodness in my unsteady amphora, hath Billy heard more heady words like "stop the war"  that hath of more perfect texture and more unceasing rise than hath while kneading the hardy batter in better times in better climes until this stink of war hath stopped the bread from rising at all, but do please, please, and yet more please, please do stop this war..

TINA  Hush, Billy, Let me handle this one or it looks hot to me. Well sir, how wilt thou the battle stop?  What is the information that thou hast unto our lady up the stairs that loveth to dress her self in the poor man's blood.

BAROBUS Telling thee awards me with not a thing. Let me meet the mother of the enemy and thou wilt be showered with gold, but until then thou seest naught, but stale bread.

TINA  Why would I care to know anyway when I can find you out from elsewhere for who from gorgeous Tina can a secret keep? You want to meet the ma'am, all right, then; come again here tomorrow, but not without the first bag of coppers, which must be my fee for naught, and Tina here, will see what she can do.

## Act 1 Scene 5

**Palace, Dubros**

ANAXARKOS

  And of benevolence, the thinking Gods

  From the seed a tree doth aim to create

  And in a timely growth build further on

  Their charge with goal of full maturity

  For in this world its fruitful place to hold,

  But, yet before that, does the man play

  god

  To his creation use as purpose to

  His greed, and in that selfish course

  destroy

  Thereof the gods created, yet did die

  Before its dignity was realised.

  It upsets me unceasingly to think

  Is it correct that some such numerous,

  Of yet fledgling years, that are but mere

  babes

  Of ten and four by us employed by right

  And for our match, who will be by us

  used,

  And on whose deaths our victories we

  will build,

  And these are the seedling boys who

  should be

  At school to grow up, support our

people,
Instead are their all ending deaths
dispatched,
And yet can I, though kingly, for them
all,
Each and every one be responsible,
When not feasible, impracticable
Is what they say it is, and are correct,
Yet neither was I born to kill and kill
Unthinkingly, without considered
thought,
And as I am no killer without cause;
The cause of wealth seems not a cause
enough,
And this the theatre of death becomes me
Not, neither is my heart in it, and nor
Can I, moored in it any pleasure find.
Yet, I will do what I can in the hope
That by mistake I can scope out the right.
(Enter the prefect with the boy)

PREFECT   My Lord, this, the grandson of the lady,

ANAXARKOS Thy name?

ELLIS                My lord, sir, my name is Ellis,.

ANAXARKOS Ellis, thou art excused from
          conscription
          To go back home, and tend thy

           grandmother.

ELLIS       She needlessly doth interferes, my lord;
           Sir, I will not leave, and she can't make
           me,
           But sir, do let me stay and fight for thee,
           My king, as did my father for thy father
           Sir, when he brave died fighting for the
           land
           As will I, sir; do let me stay on, sir.

ANAXARKOS Lad, thy father when killed was an
           adult,
           And not merely the boy of ten young
           years.

ELLIS       No, sir, my master, I will not leave thee,
           And sir, I won't go home to coward be
           And sir, my lord, thou canst not force me
           to.

ANAXARKOS Transfer this boy to my personal
           guard
           And have him wait the war out in the
           camp
           Where he will also wait the fighting out
           To then upon the war's cessation be
           Returned home; and his Nan, my
           promise kept,
           Soldier Ellis, my command disobeyed

Would be to face the chabuk,
understood?

ELLIS    Yes sir, Understand, my Lord, sir.

ANAXARKOS                    Dismissed.
(Ellis leaves.)

ANAXARKOS Mid way out seems the only way that
counts
As the sun lit night not nor moon lit day.
(Herakles enters.)

HERAKLES    Anaxarkos! I am from Axainos
To have till now with thy brothers
spoken,
But missed you while you have been
here, to find
Thee dealing death, conferring with a
child?

ANAXARKOS At times much easier are they
conferred with
Than their elders, but to see you thus
from
Axainos safely returned pleaseth me,
Giveth my worried heart respite and
hope. So Herakles, tell thou me of our
land
Sweet of olives, oranges, and honey

For which its living blood awaits be shed,
And denizens await sacrifice of
Their valuable and dispensable lives
For me that will then sit upon their
blood;
In what condition hast thou found our
home?

HERAKLES    Well, the city is quite tense and its
people
Like animals encaged are aggressive,
And distrustful of all, and me as well,
And the city's atmosphere is no more
What we knew to be the land of goodwill
That thy father ruled with not hate but
love
Who put the daily bread on each table
And good wishes upon each stranger's
lip;
But it is now a land instead that thou
Wilst know not to look upon closing
gates.

ANAXARKOS The council failed, and yes, we all
knew that
It would, but what I wish to ask thee is
That was there not peace by
other methods

By thee tried for to this skirmish end yet,
And here, by other methods, I imply
Efforts other than the council, such as,
Exampled say by our patient mother.
You met her, of course, and what did she
say?

HERAKLES    Anaxarkos, all she kept saying was
To war thou must, which now is the way
The only way that's left to her wisdom
And her sense that can redeem our land
from
This: its execrable situation.

ANAXARKOS The only way she said and these her
words?

HERAKLES    Her exact words, I have for thee to
read.

ANAXARKOS (reads) "My dear son, I implore thee
don't forget
The great injustice that is now our fate
And dissettlement now our destiny.
We, that knew not want in thy father's
rule,
Hath now been denied of not just our
land,
But are being abnegated of ourselves,
Our existence and our identity,

By being wiped away from the memory
And from the history of Axainos.
Therefore thy only task, my son, should
Buy again thyself, thy identity,
To bring back our rule upon this our land
And that is all that should thy worry be.
Think not therefore about the rights and
wrongs,
The good, the bad, the costs, the
casualties
And waste thou time not in ruminating
Whether death and war be ethical not,
But do thy duty, this thy duty is:
To fight, fight for justice and thy people,
For thy father and thy beleaguered land,
And anything that taketh thee away
From thy line of duty doth taketh thee
To turn thee wrongly away from thyself.

HERAKLES And those her very words from her to
you.

ANAXARKOS But, nowhere in these I words do I
see her,
As writing these lines and thinking these
thoughts,
For she, who was much more the thinker
than

I could mistakenly aspire to be
Who used to say that the mark of the
man
Doth lie in his ability to think
The right and wrong of every single
deed,
And to not dismiss his values as being
Secondary to aim; and then, these words
here,
Unthinking, easy words that do no work
Of thought, or of more consideration,
Than to unerringly their point arrive
In manner that she never before did
And to her mind you attribute these
words,
But in them I see her not.

HERAKLES                            You will not
See her in her visage, Anaxarkos,
Where is writ all over strain and
hardship
That her days amidst the enemy hath
Given her and erased understanding
that to security and sustainance is
Friend; but now fight this battle and
resolve
This interminable impasse is the
Only thing wherefor she has some

strength left.

ANAXARKOS What more can I say, and what more can I
        can I
        Argue when the last word on the matter
        Hath always been our mother's last
        command
        For us, her sons, and now our Gods
        forbid
        That in her distress she doth us wrongly
        Lead and guide because it is in that
        Mistaken path that her sons will move
        now
        As it's our duty to do as she bids:
        Commander and the giver of our lives,
        Shouldst know well terrain she will have
        us drive.
        (Enter the other two Sons of Ortellius)

ANSELM  A messenger from Axainos is here.

ANAXARKOS Thou thinkest that his message is of
        peace.

DION      I think not.

ANAXARKOS       Very well, but I can dare
        To hope. Call him in and have him
        narrate
        Our bloody future and otherwise

perchance.

(Enter Messenger)

ANAXARKOS It is not too late, my man, never late,
   And none too soon can thy words bring
   the peace,
   The salve that's needed to the burning in
   The enraged minds of men and women
   calm,
   And therefore speak, but speak thou
   words of peace.

MESSENGER  My message is of Aristos, my Lords
   And I the carrier be of all the wrath,
   And vitriol that drippeth from my words
   Cometh from their sender that speaketh
   no
   Peace but urgeth war and I their
   mouthpiece
   Shouldst not be smitten down for
   speaking them.

ANAXARKOS Speak ye emissary, have no fear for
   Thou art here amongst those that justice
   know.

MESSENGER Lord Aristos to Lord Anaxarkos
   Sayeth thou doth hide thy weakness and
   thy
   Cruelty in thy constant desire for peace

And sad devotion to philosophy.
Therefore stop hiding and step out to yet
Confront thy abstruse uselessness in
front
Of our employ. And, Lord Aristos, to
Dion sayeth: remember thy emboldened
Vow to show us at field thy strength and
crour,
When thou hast forgot that thou canst
hold up
Not to our green and newly fitted shoe;
And my master to Lord Anselm sayeth
Findest anew thy strength that thou hath
lost
In exile when thou rested and we fought
To gain our expertise and raise the worth
Of our son of wheels who will surpass
thee
In any confrontation that will be
And therefore drop thy quietude and
speak
Thou with the weapons to our best who
will
Become thy worst." And my lord sayeth
to
All the sons of Ortellius, "You cowards
Rise up to our challenge and from

    simp'ring
    Advocates of peace turn into real men
    And allow the rulers of Axainos
    The pleasure of taking you to your
    deaths."

HERAKLES  Tell Aristos that his words hath been
    heard,
    And their sense hath been by us
    understood,
    And to his individual speeches will
    Replies be send by us through cowardly
    Messengers not, but each reply will be
    Handed out by each one of us afield
    And not with airy words will we parley
    But by the points of each one's sword
    will each
    One answer each of thy accusations.

DION   And scamper thee away to thy master
    To say that I well remember my vow
    And tell him that Axainos' battle ground
    For the blood of Aristos' men doth
    thirsts.

ANSELM And tell him that his words frighten not
    us.

## Act 2

### The Battlefield, Axainos

CHORUS    And thus, in spite of miscarried efforts
          To resolve its growing, tumourous
          conflict
          Through peaceful means, Axainos at long
          last
          Outed its problem to the battlefield
          To turn it to a bitter clash of arms
          T'would change the heart of its restless
          landscape,
          As well the landscape of each and ev'ry
          Heart which on the restless field that day
          stood.
          The first day of the battle so arose
          That on the vast and dusty plains was
          seen
          The sun rising upon the armies twain
          And across the breach upon it that
          stretched
          Far field as the eye in the sky could see
          Stood aface each other waiting first
          strike.
          The host of Aristos' was stupendous;
          In front of which the smaller, more
          contained
          Host of Anaxarkos stood facing front,

Where Abdon and Anaxarkos did met
As the commanders of the forces twain
To settle at the center of the field
The battle's rules chartered just the same
as
All the previous battles fought, which
were that:
Shall both armies cease fighting at
sundown;
No single man by group shall be
attacked;
No person shall be struck below the
waist; Shall both the armies in full
accordance Behave with all stated virtues
such as:
Justice, truth, compassion, and honesty.
The armies did to adhere to these rules
Agree quite unaware that each and ev'ry
Single one of them would in this battle
Broken be not by one, but by both sides.
Then began the final tortuous waiting
For the call to battle to be made as
Each army shifted feet as they did see
Upon the other side the view that did
Present the enemy as their own selves:
Their friends and family and now their
foe

With whom they had lived and had
grown up with
Waited to lift their arms and to strike
them.
Friends, and relatives, and teachers,
cousins
And cases some fathers, sons, and
brothers
Stood looking on theirs as their enemy.
Anselm did look upon the other side
To see the man that in his life he cared
For most: the wrinkled face of Cyprus his
Beloved teacher that had taught him how
To the battle make, and he would now
the
Battle make with the very man that had
Imparted selflessly its wherewithal;
And then there beside him stood his
grandsire,
At whose elmed feet he had his
childhood played,
And under whose rough caresses he had
Grown up to now be taker of his life.
Anselm then did walk up to his elders
And terse with them his acquiescence
spoke
And then he turned around and then

returned
To face father not, but his enemy,
And after this, was the restless silence
Drowned by cacophony loud of trumpets
And of drums that rent the air to signal
Readiness of both armies that did then
Rush at each to battle begin.
Then with the blinking of an eye was
seen
The first collar severed from the first
head
And was seen with the merest flick of
wrist,
The first man killedeth with the first
blood spilt
Upon the dusty plains of Axainos.
The first day ended with some thousands
dead,
But no key victory for either side.
The next day too the same; the next; and
next;
For nine full days, though some hundred
thousand
Soldiers lost their lives, and yet the battle
Continued without single victory;
The reason being that on Aristos' side
His commander Abdon refused to kill

Of any son of Elowyn, instead
Daily their army weaken by killing
Thousands of unimportant cavalry,
And there on the side of Anaxarkos' did
Anselm find himself unable to cut
His grandsire down, whose aged body
was
To him yet sacred and thus inviolate.
This resulted in the ordinary
Soldiers dead, and quickly depleting
Armies, but with no major victory.
This then required the stalemate to end,
And after the ninth frustrating day,
A meeting called  in Anaxarkos' camp
Decided that there was no other way
Ahead than to Abdon strike down and
kill;
And that very night in the Aristos' camp,
Was Wesleyan with his vow taken to
Stay away from the fighting as until
Abdon did die, and therefore he did need
The old man's death same as the enemy.
The tenth day of battle the sun arose
To find Wesleyan idle in his camp
Waiting for some news to arrive that
would
End this interminable status quo.

## Act 2 Scene 1
### Battlefield, Camp of Aristos

WESLEYAN

> Is there anyone there that can hear my
> Call or is everyone the field gone to die
> Or perchance to live for what is one's
> death
> Other than another chance live anew
> In the manner that I have in staying
> From the war not killed myself but have
> chanced
> Again in the wake of Abdon's path to
> Live renewed, but what if he does not die
> That I can live and what if forever
> He drags his ancient feet to eternal
> Life and we now dead should die eternal
> And my vow to abjure this war should
> prove
> To be a grave mistake and will have me
> Interred lone in this dark and lonely
> camp
> For life. And yet away, away dark
> thoughts,
> Thou doest me no good and bringest me
> No mercy of aplomb and to thy deaths
> And banished from my mind I sendest
> thee

And in thy place must action bring
and so:
Fritz, where art thou, thou lowly knave,
thou art
To come to me at once, from whichever
Menial task might currently engage thy
Yellowing, weak and shriveled intellect.
(Enter Fritz)

FRITZ      Everyone is out in the field, my lord.

WESLEYAN As wilst thou thy pots discard to be at
My knee, thou stupid, stirring jackass,
that
Dost resent being tossed around and
dished up.
Be, thou the man god madest thee to thy
Ladle throw and take this sword, and
learn to
Stir my thrusts and here, now here at,
now here.

FRITZ      But for the field have not academy,
My Lord, I have for the kitchens been
trained.

WESLEYAN    Each one of us, thou whoreson, is in
life
Trained; art thou born to any different be
And so, my four legged trembling cat if

     Thou hath life, and here methinks within thy
     Trembles that thou must have  some, then art thou
     In its protection trained, and so there you,
     My speed is lessened and art thou allowed
     To retaliate with thy scoring knife,
     Which than the scabbard better suiteth thee:
     Now fight.

FRITZ   We have it in our kitchens, sir,
     The lord, hath sublet his command to his
     Lad Cleo, who though big is yet quite green,
     And had this your agreement is what we,
     The guards and coddlers would thou have us known.

WESLEYAN  That lord there is old his need is to
     Shield himself from Anselm's youthful assaults
     And what better way to do this than to
     Hide behind the lovers' shield and thereby
     Behind the youthful Cleo is where he

     Will his refuge find and whether I did
     Agree to this is not the concern of
     None not of thine ilk, but give lad Cleo,
     His due as marbled statue he is young,
     Attractive and appealing to the eye,
     But there his talents endeth; for Abdon
     To put Adonis quite o'er and above
     My master, I could never have agreed.

FRITZ   Wert thou in his place in command, my
     lord?

WESLEYAN What, were I in the old man's stead,
     soldier;
     For have not nine days passed us by to
     the
     Tenth that finds me still sitting here
     worse than
     Old and eunuch-like that hath sprouted
     breasts
     And manhood shrunk from inactivity:
     Hearest thou some sounds of
     celebration?

FRITZ   I do not, my lord.

WESLEYAN       Then he's still alive:
     But to want the death of someone in
     mine
     Army own and the other's victory

So that I can enter the fray looks not
Good on me that is the warrior brave
and,
That on his bottom sits to watch
others
Fight becomes me even less, and
therefore
To more practice and with less of chit
chat
Take this again to answer my parry.

FRITZ        Were you in the field right now, sir what
is
The thing you would have done to make
things move?

WESLEYAN What I would not do, thou useless
soldier,
Is to adopt a brilliant strategy
That thousands of men should be killed
each day
And their army weakened and much less
would
Call strategy for if to strategise
Was his aim then towards the
arrangement
Of the army should he have paid his
heed.

FRITZ   Arrangement of the army into what,
     My Lord, we the kitcheners would not
     know.

WESLEYAN And that slayer strong of a hundred
     men
     With a single hand hath now been
     brought down
     To this fate to soup stirrers educate:
     Well, let us see after thou hast put salt
     Thou needest know that they should put
     in
     The soldier's Alexadrine phalanx,
     Whereof its penetration, to Anselm,
     Comes easily but proves to others be
     Impossible, and a strategy is
     Built never as per our agility
     But is targeted towards their weaknesses
     And, so my trusted lad, this question
     does
     This lesson end: tell me lad what is the
     Weakness of Dion and Anaxarkos?

FRITZ :   The Alexadrine phalanx?

WESLEYAN       And the souper
     Doth superbly pass his lesson to lead
     This sorry century to salted beef.

FRITZ   And yet what about Lord Anselm's skill,

my lord?

WESLEYAN Him divert, divert is what I would do:
      To draw him farther away from the field
      Draw him afield and to remove their
      strength;
      Which is that I could have easily done
      But mental skills, they did say he hath
      not.
      How low born art thou, guard; thou
      seemest low.

FRITZ      I hold my mater in high esteem, sire.

WESLEYAN E'en if she ain't nothing but a wretched,
      Lowborn bitch that in gutter birthed thee:
      Die, thou low born, sewered, lowly scum,
      die!

FRITZ     Aaah!

WESLEYAN   Because of wimps like thee battles
      Be lost to class: go, get thyself relief.

      (Exit Fritz.)

WESLEYAN That old fool fighteth uselessly out
      there,
      Wilst I sit here useless fighting games
      Of pretence; save me Gods above, for this
      This inaction doth take my life before
      The action will be chanced to do the

same

(Enter guard.)

GUARD          My lord, my lord, that Lord Abdon has
               been
               Killed and hath Prince Aristos the
               message
               Sent thee that you are to the battle joined.

WESLEYAN Oh well, and now for me to temper the
               Exultation ' my cunning happiness
               And give the dead man his due for he
               was
               But an old man and for an old man,
               brave;
               Tell thou me, boy how came about his
               death?

GUARD          They killedeth Cleo first; then they shot
               the
               Grandsire dead.

WESLEYAN                They would need to do that,
               yes,
               But Cleomachus was armed not;
               Was he?

GUARD          Eunuch he was unarmed, my lord, and
               yet
               They shot him down unarmed and

defenseless
As there was no other way to kill the
Lord that behind his castration hideth.

WESLEYAN So that is the way that they are playing,
Is it, by the breakage of the rules; well,
So can I follow their examples not
Once but  ten times over now that they
have
Done it first and onward to the breakage
Of the until now sacred battle rules,
Watch me now enter the fray and watch
me
Now play them shot for shot and skill for
skill,

GUARD    My lord, will thou with this take o'er
command?

WESLEYAN More senior than I is Master Cyprus,
Who will now step in the place of Abdon.

## Act 2 Scene 2
### House of Hector, Axainos

BILL   But this an army of the fee-faw-fum,
      And me, the minutus, they did accost,
      To tell me that he will take me a field
      To have me take part in the fight; said I
      That I would take him apart afore he
      Doth take me, me that am so small and
      whom
      They believe they needed to rug the field
      For what was my question. Would it be
      to
      Bake; his answer was to the fires feed.
      Didst thou hear that Tina love, I that till
      Now fed the fires will now fires feed.
      I then him asked that who will come with
      me:
      To which he did say not the rugged Tom
      for
      He is here needed and not the neat lass
      Tina either, for the dugs are exempt,
      And so the answer is plain simple that
      A sister frail I'll be to escape death,
      For Billy, nay Bella, bodily weak
      But her brains can never be found
      wanting
      And therefore, dear Tina, dear  sister

mine

Good friend and almond kind, do give to me

Thy skirt to my endangered manhood hide

And stay the fate of which I'm terrified.

(Enter Barobus)

TINA  Yes, all right, and therefore, thou deflated lump of pretentious cake batter after having imparted to thee thy position in this household I now have  to meet someone that I am sure cometh with more that thou hath, or will ever have and that thy prattling can ever me offer so take thyself away from here, Billyboy immediately, and leave us alone.

(Exit Billy)

TINA  Yes, and hast thou anything with thee that might make it worth my while?

BAROBUS Well I have these.

TINA  These coins to our health are but trinkets that doth cover not quarter of what I have for thee, which is information that for long now hath she been desperately searching for a scribe but to no avail. So thought I if I let thee in as a scribe the duration of her search and desperation of her need will reduce her doubt of my endeavour, and therefore as thou canst see we, the servants of the House of Hector, cometh not cheap and will have our palms graced with more grease than is what you have here.

BAROBUS The rest comes later.

TINA   Had I not enmity with her I would never settle for what are but fallen scraps that are lifted not to grace the table of a rich man's maid, but I am in hunger for revenge, therefore hast thou any skill with the quill?

BAROBUS Quill, my quill?

TINA   Not very well spoken art thou, soldier; I meant of writing, skill of writing, to pass off as the scribe, and waste thee not my time with thy ribaldry.

BAROBUS Let me in as the scribe and if need be I will show her my skill with my quill.

TINA   And there, she doth come hither.

(Enter Elowyn)

TINA        My Lady, if you could give me some of
            thy time for the Lord Hector hath you
            were looking for a scribe, and that I was
            to make enquiries and I have for you
            here who may be able to help.

ELOWYN  I did need one, and you must be the
            scribe.

BAROBUS  If the warp's abb seems not dull then I
            must.

ELOWYN  (to Tina) Thou may leave us with him,
            and I thank thee.
            A formal referral is not allowed
            And even so thy title we accept
            For thy demeanour seems to be learned.

BAROBUS  There seems to be no passport to the quill
            Just as the bobbin passes naught between
            The warp and weft that toillinette creates.

ELOWYN  Yes, whatever sense that remark might
            make,
            But we will to work, which I will
            describe
            As the writing of records that have by
            Absolutism unwritten, and razed,
            And that need to be rebuilt and restored:
            First will be the truth of Axainos' rule,

The truth of King Ortellius' rule  that
spans
All of thirty years to include the truth
Of me as queen and future kings, my
sons.

BAROBUS  Your sons?

ELOWYN      Of what did you not
understand.

BAROBUS  The Sons of Ortellius?

ELOWYN       Why yes.

BAROBUS        And here
I would ask thee how many are they
these
The sons of Ortellius and here I hear
Thee silenced as if thou hast  understood
My implication not, which was about
Thy sons: they number only three, no
more,
But what about thine other son, the
fourth,
whose truth, alas, hath been to history
lost
Because it mattered, no, not ever did
Matter to thee that thy fourth is
unknown

And now if thou disregardest him thus:
Why shouldst thy truth to the ages
matter?

ELOWYN  Thou art?

BAROBUS                  Know ye not, I am, he, thy son.

ELOWYN  Who hath let this man inside? Guard!
Sergei.
(The man escapes. Enter Sergei.)

ELOWYN  Sergei, there was this man here just now.

SERGEI  Shall I have him yet pursued, my lady?

ELOWYN  Is he all gone, then maybe not just now
When I will to Hector have it taken.
Instead now I'll have thee tell me of the
Events that at the field occurred this day.

SERGEI  We have it just that the newly entranced
Wesleyan has now begun his battle
And to inflict destruction upon us.

ELOWYN  Yes, well that is all I had to know if
Wesleyan hath begun to fight but his
Effect on our army is best worried
By my sons and is not my concern at
This time and so tell thou the master he
should give me attendance immediately
So that I can his assistance obtain

To solve this newly presented problem.
No sooner does one try to solve one case
Is another one by nature added
Which then does divide one's
application,
And one's efforts to one's disquiet
double
And reduce much needed effectiveness
Of application exercised elsewhere;
So Sergei to Lord Hector to tell him
That he should come here for me
straightaway.

## Act 2 Scene 3

### Camp of Anaxarkos, Battlefield.

HERAKLES   And even so the war, Anaxarkos,
     Is this hell heated theatre of death, not
     The most normal of situations in
     Which the quick tempers of each one and their
     Acerbities are to be mirrored not
     But born out patiently and do with both
     Anselm and Dion barter kind patience for
     Their short behaviour and stressful talk.

ANAXARKOS But Herakles, on this day of all which
     Although seemed like all the other battle
     Days, and yet it brought upon my heart a
     Most deep and terrifying sense of dread
     And danger signaling that fight today
     Might out of control spiral into an
     Unknown state of peril, but before I
     Could convey it to my brothers I have
     Found that Anselm is left early before
     The sun hath rised, and Dion is otherwise
     Engaged and why was this told not to me?

HERAKLES   Anselm was the sure call of valour
     sent

By the Tigranes for which he hath left,
But as to the reason why did not meet
With thee is that you barely talk to them
But to scold them and they do same to
thee.
(Dion comes in)

DION        Anaxarkos.

ANAXARKOS                        Dion, listen to me
When I tell thee that this last day's battle
Numbered way too many dead and this
day
Needs must the living have to control
them.

DION        No, brother, no, a debate with thee on
Philosophy is not the action that
Necessitates the day, and thou will for
A change listen to me what I have which
Is that they have sat down to a meeting
Last night whereat they have decided on
The Alexandrine in the day's battle
And this when, we have not Anselm with
us.

ANAXARKOS Out, the horror of the premonition:
Call back Anselm if it be not too late.

DION        Nay, not possible, he hath gone too far

Afield to call him back , but loss of face
And therefore to some other method of
Retaliation, and I wondered on
My way here whether I could myself in
Any unlettered way attack hard the
Lead against them straight onto their
phalanx.

HERAKLES    It is not the matter of thy knowledge
Which by lack of permission hath been
not
Granted thee for those that are not in the
League of Anselm are forbidden to the
Alexandrine break and to flout this rule
Would be to call on wrath divine, besides
Which we already with infringement
have
Been charged at this war's trite
beginning.

ANAXARKOS It was their strategy then: to absent
Anselm wherewith sans him to helpless
us.

HERAKLES    Onward to some other more of
defense
Then, Dion, my man and what more
have ye there?

DION       Anaxarkos, do not make us helpless

By calling us so, and Herakles, we
Have to face the phalanx without Anselm
Is all there is to it and we can do
So in two ways: one is by using force,
Brute force, which to my mind is the
better.

ANAXARKOS Never.

HERAKLES                The only way, it seems to me.

ANAXARKOS Not the way I choose: the use of force
                in
                Cases such as these rarely succeedeth,
                And more over would it cause the deaths
                of
                Fifty thousand needed people at least.

DION            More than that number, brother, that's
                for sure,
                As will re-closure of the opening made
                By force be hindered with some sufficient
                Deaths, but in the words of philosophy:
                "Is death not another word for war?;"
                Do we at war have any other choice.

ANAXARKOS Two options, thou didst said; this is
                one then
                Let me hear the other, second option.

DION            The second option is young Anius, who

Being the son of Anselm also hath the
Hushed permission of their secret league.

ANAXARKOS But that is perfect for young Anius hath
Been the procedure taught by his father.

HERAKLES Not full; he hath been taught the
method half,
And only half, wherewith he can go in,
But cannot come out of that entrapment
Whereof Anselm did teach him not for he
At fourteen is in years  too childlike yet
And consider this: if he did enter
By breaking the formation, but could not
Come out then it would mean a certain
death;
Said, "half the knowledge is a dangerous
thing".

ANAXARKOS Half the knowledge is but all that we
need:
For the formation once made open by
Anius, will be by our army quick
plugged
Immediately, without delay, and will its
Reclosure be by us quite disallowed
Which will make his knowledge's lack to
exit

Entirely unnecessary, and this
May be the better option of the two.

DION  The better option for it doth in the
Mind's eye seem all neat and quite
possible,
But in reality is way of risk
And alarm wherein a child without the
Experience of the world, will face the
might
Of the imperial army all alone.

ANAXARKOS He will face Aristos' army, yes, but
He will not be alone but will ride in
Fore front of our entire army, that will
Support him with experience, and why
should
That be not to good effect because where
Anselm sometimes stumbles out of a fear
And doubt, Anius never does that's how
Capable he is and that's how much
brave.

DION  The certainty you have about this, sir,
I can match it not for, gods forbid that
Anything should happen to young
Anius,
Anselm will us all hold responsible.

ANAXARKOS Accuse me not of certainty, Dion

|  |  |
|---|---|
|  | As the only thing that I am certain |
|  | Of is that I cannot risk the deaths of |
|  | More soldiers, but responsibility |
|  | Thou canst solely put upon my shoulders |
|  | As being the eldest, am responsible |
|  | For everything that happens in this war, |
|  | For every life and every death; be it |
|  | That of any ordinary soldier, |
|  | Or of my son that is still young in years. |
| DION | All right then, the trumpets summon us to |
|  | Field to which we should proceed, but not 'fore |
|  | I brief Anius then we will to war. |
|  | (All except the guards leave.) |
| ELLIS | I will also to the field and to war. |
| PREFECT | Thou wilst stay right here; those are mine orders. |
| ELLIS | When Anius fights, why does Ellis not? |
| PREFECT | Anius hath a year more than thou hast |
|  | And besides he is the son of Anselm. |
| ELLIS | Anius hath the same years as have I |
|  | And besides if he the son of Anselm |
|  | Is then am I not my father's son for |
|  | Both Lord Anselm and my father hath |

war

Anius hath the same then why not me?

PREFECT　Bantling then, give thy mouth a rest, and
take
One step outside this camp would be to
ask
Me to thee put upon my knee and give
To thee the lesson of a strapping sound.
Get thou within and sing thou praises to
One that's gifted thee thy miserable
Life and cease thy whining; in thou gets
thee.

## Act 3

### The Battlefield

CHORUS   And thus did the events of that morning
           Of the thirteenth day bring up its dawn
           to
           Tempt its fate into the makings of shame
           And the hanging of its head, and the sun
           Arose to the magnificent expanse
           Of the smart formation by Wesleyan
           Created as target for a mere boy,
           A small boy facing the army large and
           Inexperience tackling imperial
           Might and whether Anaxarkos' ploy
           would
           Work was anybody's guess when the boy
           First a rode the field and was seen by all.

           But he saw not any other than the
           Enemy with his uncle Dion's words
           Still ringing in his ears telling him to
           The army lead that day and do as his
           Father would have done the phalanx
           break.
           The fledgling son of Anselm had agreed
           To do as he was told and there he was:
           That day a small and a nervous leader.

He then kicked his horse to begin his ride
Towards the formation with fear in his
Heart slight and mixed with the still
excitement
Of the moment that resulted in an
Intoxicating memory of his
Father's teaching, which was at the onset
Thou shouldst focus on the task ahead
and
Free thy mind from all excess emotion,
And as Anius did approach the front
He calmed his mind, and freed it from all
wild
Excitement to have control in its place:
Calmness of the mind, firmness of
resolve.

Anius then looked at his target and
Remembered every instruction that he
By his father had been taught and
schooled in
Wherewith he did advance upon the
phalanx
And in their very sight he did create
A momentary agitation in
The army of Aristos, that lead to
An expert piercing of the formation

And deft breakage made for an opening
Enough so that his back up support of
The army could him follow, and as was
Planned the soldiers rushed towards this
entrance
But e'en before one of Anaxarkos'
Soldiers could this entrance enter  it was
Found in astonishment by them that the
Access availed them vanished suddenly.

The rushing soldiers stopped and was
there the
Momentary confusion amongst the
Men of Anaxarkos afore there came
Realisation that the entrance by the
Boy created had been closed by whom
they
At that point of time knew not, but it
stopped
The men milled outside the closed
formation
Lost in their confusion and uselessness
The while that their young warrior was
inside
Trapped and from them cut off quite
completely.

Past the crowd of the opposing army
Stood Anius sole, who around him
looked to find
On all the sides of him were soldiers of
The enemy whereof not one of them
Could be relied upon and whereof all
Needed to be fended off and he at
Once realised what had occurred and
that
He was entirely trapped and on his own,
And with that realisation came that what
Needed now was to fight and so, he
raised
His weapons fought in manner of a
young
Wild cat, not wasting time in thought or
fear
Of death, but lashing out on all the sides
To hurt, to maim, to slash, kill anyone
Or anything that came too close with just
One aim: to keep the enemy distance
Safe and well away from his lone body.

Amongst the enemy were there some
that
Dared to think an easy victim was the
Young trapped boy and that advanced

upon him
To later boast about, but they only
Fell to the fury of sword of Anius.
Amongst those that fell was Wesleyan's
son,
Whom Anius did treat like he had all the
rest
Deftly and swiftly to their deaths upon
The ground, and when Wesleyan saw his
boy
Killed he did to the master Cyprus ride
To ask him which the best way was to
send
The son of Anselm off and the master
Said the longer that the bow stayed in the
The hands of Anius. the son of Anselm
Would stay unbeatable, and thereby did
Wesleyan take it upon himself to
Weaken the lad and take him to this
death.
It was a match unequal not in years
Alone, but also in experience
And skill, with the only thing that Anius
Had above Wesleyan was ignorance:
The confidence of youth that bothered
not
With probability, but mustered onto

Fight. Thus did Anuis answer each of the
Attacks three wherein when Wesleyan
killed
His steed, the boy fought on from his
fallen
Chariot; and when Wesleyan brought
down his
Chariot, the boy fought from the ground
level;
And when Wesleyan from his hand did
cut
His spear the boy took up the broken
wheel
From his fallen chariot with which he did
Defend himself; and when did come his
death
In the form of the final attack to kill
The body of Anius was overcome,
But his defiance stayed intact until
The moment that his breath his body left,
And then, and only then, the boy of not
More than ten and four, did fall to
ground, dead.

## Act 3 Scene 1
### Anaxarkos' Camp, Axainos

MALACUS     How terrible was the day's fight, how terrible, and how good it is to be back to this camp, so tired we are all, so tired but safe.

ELLIS     How was it? Do tell. What happened? Didst thou see him go in? Didst thou see the door close? Who hath the formation closed? Dost thou know? Tell me for I want to know.

MALACUS     Terrible, it was and so terrible, but you look so clean and safe here in this camp, and we so tired for out there in the field have we been all sfighting and slipping on the bloodied ground.

ELLIS     But who closed the formation and was it the King of Sophene? They said in the kitchens that it was Sophene

MALACUS     We all saw Anius go in.

ELLIS     Thou didst see him then?

MALACUS     And here was I ready to rush in after him as were we all, but then we all saw the door shut, and, oh but it was much too terrible; lucky art thou to have escaped it all.

ELLIS      Lucky, but I do not want that kind of
luck. I want to fight and I will come with
thee for the next battle.

MALACUS    Against the King's orders?

ELLIS      But I will disobey my King not to
disobey, but to fight and I will fight.
(Enter Anaxarkos, Dion, and Herakles.
Exit Malacus and Ellis.)

DION       But it is not possible he could have
Uttered that and for certain hath this
report
Been misconstrued and misrepresented.

HERAKLES    Anselm is a grieving father, Dion.

DION       But he's foremost a warrior, Herakles!

HERAKLES    Yet what exactly hath been detailed
and,
What are they saying he hath vowed to
do?

DION       That he will Zaradrus eradicate
Or else, lay down  arms which is another
Way of saying that he will give up the
Battle; we do not on no grounds concede
Victory, no matter how high is the

Human cost and no matter how many
Of our near and dear have perished the
fray.

HERAKLES   He hath from some emotion made this
vow.

DION   Emotional and Anselm, never, no,
For Anselm hath never been emotion's
Slave and now perchance the news is
true will
They behind a strong defense ensure the
Safety of Zaradrus and will they just
Wait for the sun to set and for Anselm
To have lost his vow and lay down his
arms;
After which have they won this war
without
Having tried or fought too much for their
gains
Because of Anselm's rashness and his
vow
What more is needed now to win by
them?

PREFECT   My Lords, Lord Anselm hath entered the
camp.

DION   Be ready all of ye to talk to him:
If indeed he hath truly uttered it,

    Then make him see the senselessness of
    his
    Vow and force him to retract it, or else,
    At least, make him to change and alter it!

HERAKLES  Once gi'en one's word is abidance
    stated;
    I doubt he can do nought but follow
    through.
    (Anselm enters)

ANSELM  Anaxarkos, tell me the reason and
    What transpired to have my son killed by
    thee.

ANAXARKOS Anselm…

ANSELM     And had I known that you
    send small
    Boys to their deaths, that my boy was
    unsafe
    And would be by thee sent afield and
    killed.

ANAXARKOS Anselm...

ANSELM     Or should I blame myself
    because
    Although I knew thee weak, irresolute
    And cowardly, with you I entrusted
    The safety of my son and went away

Assured to answer my enemies' call.

DION　　Brother.

ANSELM　　　　　All of you, all of you have to
His death my son sent and I will
avenge…
But no, forgive me for I am distraught,
And blame on ye the fault that lies upon
The Zaradrus that hath the lifeline cut
And trapped my darling strappling
inside it
Alone surrounded by the enemy
And caught whenst must he have
thought that now my
Father will arrive now any moment
Now, when he will come and save me
from this
Must his final thought have been, alas, it
Was not so, and he scared died all alone.

DION　　Anselm it was…

ANSELM　　　　　　This grief doth cut me
like
A sword; its edge, its pain doth screams
to me
The killing of my son avenge or else
Will I direct its edge in severance of
This my own and useless life that deigns

to

Out the son after whom it flaccid lives.

DION        Anselm!

ANSELM                          And yet, if I convert
            the pain
            Into action then towards the King of
            Sophene must I divert my wrath and
            make
            Him feel its knife's edge at his neck and
            look
            Upon the face of death in manner that
            He my young son made, and therefore,
            list'n
            As I declare to you the vow I've made.

DION        Forbear, no, Anselm, no.

ANSELM                          And my vow is
            That by the next sundown will, Zaradrus
            Be killed and if I fail, will I lay down
            My weapons and mine arms, and that is
            all
            That I have left to say; forgive thou me
            My emotional indulgence and the next
            Time I will speak when vengeance of my
            son's
            Killing hath been accomplished and
            achieved.

(Exit Anselm)

HERAKLES    He is not in faculty of his sense.

DION        Are we too not in faculty of our
            Senses that we could not talk to him, but
            Then again, in face of his loud grief what
            Could we have said, and now instead to
            the
            Enemy all we have to say is this
            "Here on this guilded platter we present
            To thee the throne and the crown as our
            gifts
            From us, the losers of this battle that
            Could not the cost of deaths endure and
            that
            Are not fit to rule as kings; say something
            Herakles, find us a way out of this
            Situation that we have ourselves in.

HERAKLES    Alright, we have only one way ahead
            Of us and that way is to ensure that
            Anselm completes his vow and Zaradrus
            Kills definitely and without fail by
            The sun down at the morrow, which to
            my
            Mind is our only option and therefore
            To ensure his death is our single task.

DION        Very well then, that is good to hear and

Quite the start and quite alright and
much fine,
Much better and so now that we know
our
Single task, we need to know how we
must
Accomplish it and how to encertain
That the king of Sophene dies tomorrow.

HERAKLES   That I would have thee leave to me
when I
Will accompany Anselm unto the field
Tomorrow, to his chariot drive, to guide
Him along the steps of each way; and
now
Proceed, let go, Anaxarkos, what say?

ANAXARKOS I'll be with thee presently, Herakles.
(Herakles and Dion leave. Prefect enters.)

PREFECT  My Lord, thou hadst commanded me to
bring
Ellis the boy to speak with thee, my lord.

ANAXARKOS We must not have him at the action's
face.

PREFECT  My Lord, that I have everywhere for him
Looked but he hath disappeared and
when I

Find him will he for this disobedience be
Punished and brought at once before
thee made.

ANAXARKOS Leave him be for the moment and
answer
Me this: dost thou remember that day the
Old woman came to see me?

PREFECT                                    Yes, my lord.

ANAXARKOS What sayeth her to us that day when
we
Did grant to her her grandson: that my
hands
Will be stained with blood, my own
brother's blood,
My brother whom she said that I will
kill?

PREFECT  She doth rant e'en now in the square,
m'lord.

ANAXARKOS Ever hath she predicted correctly?

PREFECT  But she is an old and raving hag, please
Place ye no weightage upon her  toothy
Words that are mixed with aged sputum
hath no
Sense and neither allegiance, my good
Lord

ANAXARKOS I see thee shade thine eyes yet tell it
   Me straight, soldier,: hath she or hath she
   not
   Made predictions that became true,
   before?

PREFECT She hath, my lord and they do call her
   witch.
   (Enter Herakles)

HERAKLES Prefect, leave. Anaxarkos…

ANAXARKOS        Herakles,
   A while when I would like to speak with
   ye
   In solitude; now about  how Anselm
   Did behave just dispossessed by his grief
   Completely in a manner that he did
   Never do before and in this state of
   Mind, will he face the morrow's enemy
   To what, perchance to his death? Do tell
   me,
   At the morrow will I Anselm kill in
   The manner that today I killed his son?

HERAKLES Come away from these thoughts,
   Anaxarkos
   That nothing, but crippling remorse
   achieve.

ANAXARKOS I try but shed them not nor walk
away,
For my inability to war with
My brothers cripples me, and the more
blood
I shed of others more bleed I myself
And do weaken so much that I cannot
Move nor think nor feel, and in this sad
state
Must I at the morrow the battle face?

HERAKLES    Tomorrow's fate will be at 'morrow
fought
For today to be bought yet doth awaits
And come thou now to where we expect
ye
For Dion will not without thee proceed.

## Act 3 Scene 2
### Aristos' camp.  Axainos

WESLEYAN Celebrations, celebrations, let us,
Have more celebrations; who have we
here
Pretty carafe, golden lad, we welcome
Thee that cometh sooner than expected
Like a couquet with a promise at his
Lips and perchance deadly dagger
girded
To his tense thigh, but out frail doubt for
thou
Dost scare us not with thy slight
disbelief;
For there she is from beyond the pale that
Shines her rays upon us to adorn our
Head with her celestial coronet of
Golden sunshine and itself does station
Behind us like the divine cabochon.
What more is now needed to proclaim
thou
Of all that thou perceivest art the king
And thy rule is forever more secured.

ARISTOS   Fie thy wordiness, my friend, Wesleyan,
For that we have won seems
disbelieving.

WESLEYAN This battle is already history
As is thy success already assured
For when the sun will shine its head at
dawn
What's left is to collect the spoils that are
By their folly us assigned already
By which our victory is as of now
Encertained and by sun down next all
that
Remains the already dead disputers
To inter, and with them their wrong and
their
Persistent dispute be fore'er buried.
(Enter Norman)

NORMAN Nay, Brother not so for we have trouble:
I bring news that Zaradrus will leave the
Battle and and he hath already with the
Master spake that bid me take thee to the
Deserter to sort the matter with him.

WESLEYAN That white-lilly livered, misbegotten,
Whoreson wants to leave now, our
assured win?

ARISTOS  Wesleyan, please; what hath transpired,
Norman?

NORMAN  He is frightened of the vow of
Anselm.

WESLEYAN   In our moment of victory does that
                      Irritating jelly jaw want to leave?

ARISTOS   He will not after  I have spake with him.

WESLEYAN And I will come with you to sort him
                      out.

ARISTOS   A while Wesleyan, for you knoweth that
                      Zaradrus hates ye as a dying lamp
                      Doth hate the ever shining, brilliant sun,
                      And therefore must you here wait whilst
                      I speak
                      With him alone to better persuade
                      Him into staying for tremulous he
                      Maybe, but warrior that is entirely
                      Necessary for tomorrow's battle.

WESLEYAN Very well then.

ARISTOS                                       And thus art thou, as a
                      Lover and an artist, upset, but trust
                      In me brother, for if I find myself
                      Failing to hold him back I will call for
                      Thee, but for now let's pretend that the
                      red
                      Rising is his passion, and thou art the
                      Fading fire; Norman, stay thou with him.
                      (Aristos leaves.)

NORMAN What doest thou?

WESLEYAN                    Shine my sword.

NORMAN                                    Is it not
        Shined enough, it seems gleaming to
        mine eye?

WESLEYAN The more I shine it more I see the face
        In it of mine enemy for it's not
        As though I cannot see that they have on
        Purpose forced his hand to tremble and
        have
        Shaken him into leaving the battle
        And have because of it again spread fight
        And distrust between Aristos and me.

NORMAN If they have done this on purpose then
        they
        May yet fail because from here I see that
        Aristos doth speaks to Zaradrus and
        On the shoulder of the rat  I see from
        Here the placative arm of my King
        placed,
        And now does Master Cyprus join them
        but,
        What they speak of I can only guess from
        Gesticulations of that wordy coward
        And by the manner in which with his
        hands
        And his white and trembling face he

doth urge,
Beseech, and plead, and entreat Aristos.

WESLEYAN Norman, look away a while, and tell
me
Here that I wish to know: does Aristos
Not trust me and has he ever taken
Thee into his confidence to tell thee
Anything other than I am loyal
To him and owe him all I am and own.

NORMAN That he doth know.

WESLEYAN　　　　　　　　　Then must he know
that I
Would never do to his hurt his interest.
(Enter Aristos and Cyprus.)

ARISTOS　Why so afeard? What's wrong with the
man?

CYPRUS　Anyway, for the time being, at least, have
We succeeded to his departure stay,
And now Prince Aristos I take thy leave,
For the sun will at the horizon be;
The day's apparailyng is yet half done.

ARISTOS　Yes, the hour is now well past the night.
Norman, go with the master 'cross the
camp.
(Exit Cyprus and Norman)

WESLEYAN Hath that running rat agreed to stay
       on?

ARISTOS   He was all set to leave, and return to
       His kingdom for he said that he hath fear
       Of dying sure in the morrow's battle.

WESLEYAN Fear of dying! And if he stays then does
       He think that he will not be protected
       When he doth knows and we did tell him
       that
       His position in the battle 'morrow
       Remaineth unassailable; didst thou
       Tell that stupid idiot that?

ARISTOS                           Yes, we did.

WESLEYAN That we have kept his worthless self
       safely
       Guarded like helpless newborn babe in
       Forces womb where he's protected by me
       And my guard primarily at the front,
       Behind whom will be stationed Leroy's
       force,
       And then will be the Nicomedes, and
       then
       The Nicostratii and the Tigranii,
       Behind them hundred thousand cavalry,
       Followed by twenty thousand hoplites
       And then there at the distance of twelve

miles
Will Zaradrus be, way beyond, within
The safety and security of our
Defense will he be placed and even then
Sayeth he that he has a fear of death?

ARISTOS Of course, but we did reassure him of
this
When was his reply that no matter what
May our preparations be, the one thing
That he knows and fears is if Anselm has
Vowed to kill him, it will be so done in
One way or another, and he also
Said for it is Anselm's vow we speak of
And not an empty vow of Wesleyan.

WESLEYAN That I have vowed to kill Anselm, I
will;
Doth that fact make to him no difference?

ARISTOS Wesleyan, the trust that we have in you
They, the allies have not as they see that
Which you show them, while we see and
know that
Thou art beyond thy appearance's show
But tell me what hath upset thee; is it
Zaradrus wanted not to meet with thee?

WESLEYAN His vain desires matter nothing to me.

ARISTOS   Know importance of the morrow's battle
          Can be stated not enough and wherefore
          His presence is important and a must.

WESLEYAN Aristos, tomorrow's battle is of
          Concern tomorrow when I have vowed
          to
          Kill Anselm since the day that I was
          born.

ARISTOS   That is true, but we still need Zaradrus.

WESLEYAN My king you need no one other than I.

ARISTOS   Yes, Wesleyan; all right; whether we
          have
          Zaradrus or not, as long as we have
          Thee, we have the certain death of
          Anselm
          And we have assured victory at hand:
          Is that not what you wanted me to say?

WESLEYAN For that very reason I was birthed.

ARISTOS   So then thou wilst Anselm kill
          tomorrow?

WESLEYAN Because I am to the charioteer born
          The others hate me, but my friend, my
          Lord
          Let me not have that kind treatment from
          you.

ARISTOS   Of course not, thou whoress's son; come,
          let us
          Pass the remainder of this night in drink
          And by the shining of the wine our next
          Day's certain checkmate think wherein
          the sun
          Will o'er the board depart and the pieces
          Of their revolt return as boxed for good .

## Act 3 Scene 3
### House of Hector, Axainos

HECTOR   Things are all alright, sister, look thou
not
So worried for he hath been caught
passed out
From drink in the tavern, where as mere
wretch,
And a petty thief, an extortioner
Of money was he called out and brought
here
In an inebriated state for thee
To dispense with as thou doth see it fit.
(Enter Sergei)

SERGEI   My Lady, we have held the man outside
When would you like us to bring him
hither?

ELOWYN   A while, Sergei, waitest thou awhile
when
Hector, I would speak with thee about
his
Immurement which if not planned in
advance
And with care we will much trouble face
for
He may be quite common in his present

Circumstance and yet may prove to hence

Threaten proceedings.

HECTOR                            Dangerous, but how?

ELOWYN   It will be clearer when we question him,
But I know already he may a tense
The situation further, and therefore
May be needed to be kept under lock
And key; far from the palace as is meet.

HECTOR   First  he should be interviewed to know which
Mode of imprisonment will suit us best.

ELOWYN   Very well, then. Guard! Have the man brought in.
(Sergei brings the scribe in.)

HECTOR   What is thy name?

BAROBUS                   My name is Wesleyan.

ELOWYN   What is it that thou knowest about him?

BAROBUS Know I not all about myself for that
Is who I am: I am him, Wesleyan.

HECTOR   He definitely is drunk but maybe
He is also a bit off his senses?

BAROBUS I am as I am and I am as dried
And browned as the  bark of a thirty tree,

    Whose parchment yearns for a sip, nay a drop
    Of wine to slake my thirst I ask of ye,
    And I plead with ye, some succor, dried thirst.

HECTOR First tell us what thou know then thy receipt.

BAROBUS And money, yes, thou wilt me money give.

HECTOR For thy knowledge, first

BAROBUS         I am Wesleyan?

HECTOR Thou art not.

BAROBUS    Then who am I; do tell me?

ELOWYN Awhile, and let me handle this Hector;
    Let us our thoughts level with his for being
    An animal will teach us to trap one,
    And yes, therefore prisoner, allow me
    To introduce thyself to thee and yes,
    Thou art Wesleyan; and now do tell us
    About who thou art and of thy desires.

BAROBUS My hand, Wesleyan's hands shakes for 'ere I
    Could at the tavern pick the cup they

threw
Me out. I want a weapon with my wine.

ELOWYN  But, first thou must tell us about thyself.

BAROBUS  Wesleyan, I am that, but no, not the
Warrior that people knoweth, for he
A Charioteer's son is not, but I am not
That, I am the warrior people knoweth
Not, as the son of Elowyn and that
Is who I'm, Wesleyan, Elowyn's Son.
Elowyn, art thou; art thou Elowyn
And didst thou not birth Wesleyan, that's
me
Before thou birthed Anaxarkos, there -
That in horror thou dost away, but
Thy face answers my question that thou
didst
Birth me worthless, as thy girl womb's
mistake
To from thy breasts be wrenched and
cast into
Hapless wilds in untethered infancy
And be adopted by one that would drive
My circumstances and identity
Yet Elowyn, yet you did birthed me,
Forget thou not Xenarchus for my name
Is Xenarchus, son of Elowyn, whom

By thy wanton and thy sore Nature made
High born Xenarchus to low Wesleyan.

HECTOR He is deranged.

BAROBUS      … and of whom, bad
lady
Pray tell me that to whom wast thou, the
whore,
To which cuckold, didst thou give thy
maiden
Self, mine father, name of which I know
not.

ELOWYN He continues his speech under breath.

HECTOR Speak louder, man.

BAROBUS      Thou didst keep this
secret
Of me from mine younger half brothers
three
Anaxarkos, Anselm and Dion, that
Consider me their avowed foe and a
Charioteer's son, but the truth will out
from
Under the skirts of the guilty whoress
When I tell them that "Your eldest
brother,
Xenarchus is who I am; end this war!";

Anaxarkos will end this war and he
Will hand to me the throne and I will like
The new son rise to all the kingdom rule
As the king of Axainos and then,
And then, thou lowly woman, whence
the proud
Owner of all this world's wealth, will I
Then, make you pay for what you did to
me
But that for a later day, for now wine
I beseech ye, my killer thirst to slake.

HECTOR   Give him wine to drink and Wesleyan,
tell
Me how didst thou come to know of all
this?

BAROBUS At the Pontus edge.

ELOWYN                    That is enough. Guard.

BAROBUS Why didst thou abandon me, mine
mother.
Mother, mine, why and  throw me afire,
why?
(Sergei takes him away)

HECTOR   You did hide his speech, sister, just when
he
Was about to tell us from whereby he

Came to hear this that he threatens us
with .

ELOWYN  That later, but first, now thou knowest
that
The havoc he can raise and that in a
Saga already fraught with fright create
With more delay in the proceedings more
Unhappiness and deaths, so must thou
Decide the best that thou canst do to him.

HECTOR  Kill him I don't think, for unless like
some
Criminals we the bury body in
The night's dark, to avoid disclosure and
Then we must face the rumours of our
deed
That despite our efforts will the palace
Reach sooner or later to suspicion
Raise with doubts about my neutrality.

ELOWYN  What then?

HECTOR                              Until the battle, we
detain
Him in the stronghold basement of this
house.

ELOWYN  Good, that is what we must do at once
then.

HECTOR    Guard, have the prisoner to cells below
          And imprisoned until  further orders.
          (Sergei leaves)

HECTOR    And now sister, why didst thou cut him
          off
          Just when he was to tell us of what hath
          Transpired at the sacred Pontus' waters.

ELOWYN    Hear it from me and thou may hear more
          sense:
          I met Wesleyan the real Wesleyan
          By the Pontus' waters' edge when this
          man,
          The deranged thief must have overheard
          my
          Private conversation with my son.

HECTOR                                     When?

ELOWYN    Before the war began, and soon after
          Herakles with him did speak to convince
          Him and failed, I thought that if I spoke
          with
          Him myself, I would the better faire.

HECTOR    And what was it you said to Wesleyan?

ELOWYN    My aim was to see for myself this man,
          My first born, although aware his
          brothers

And his enemies are one and the same
Who nothing wants more than to shed
our blood
And to end all our lives; nay my aim was
Not so much to meet my selfish son that
No stranger is to me, but to bring some
Stature to this awful statelessness of
Affairs that Axainos finds itself in?

HECTOR  Do tell what hath transpired at the
meeting?

ELOWYN  By the waters of the seas, and with its
Undulating reflections on us both,
Mother and son, did I, as Herakles
Did before me, tell him to change sides
and
As he did Herakles, he refused
My proposal, as well.

HECTOR                                What else transpired.

ELOWYN  I lost my nerve, Hector with one that is
My eldest, in whom our blood is most
strong
And who is of us most intelligent,
But beyond that, I lost my nerve because
Having a lot to hate me for  he is
More ruthless, and does not need to try
too

Hard at all to kill all my sons not once
But many times over.

HECTOR                                    What more happened?

ELOWYN  I entreated him with my hands folded
          And pleaded with the eldest to the lives
          Of his younger brothers spare, and in
          that
          I think, I did no wrong, but more pride in
          Him exists than his status does allow
          And that day with his head held way
          above
          Mine, too high, in the manner that I
          should
          Have expected, in all his pride he said
          That as I had come to him and pleaded
          With him, he could not send me away
          with
          Nothing in my hands, and he did
          promise
          Me that he would spare two of the
          brothers.

HECTOR  Why, this I cannot believe, but did he
          Say that he would spare the lives of your
          sons?

ELOWYN  Not all my sons, but of Anaxarkos
          And Dion, whose lives he said would

proudly spare,
But Anselm he would fight to kill to
death.

HECTOR  This bodes not well.

ELOWYN           But why, what be thy fear?

HECTOR  Thou hast not fairly played, sister, for by
Working on his emotions and his pride,
You have forced him to save the lives of
two
And at the same time he hath broken not
His allegiance to Aristos; and is
Now in the middle trapped along with
him
Are we all in the middle trapped because
Of this promise thou hast solicited.

ELOWYN  Be this not a war, my lord, that it be
Coloured black or white; it be coloured
fair?

HECTOR  And yet, sister, even in this war, which,
Yes, does validate everything that's fair,
Hast thou caused even its implacable
Brow, otherwise of all forms of evil
Injustice forgiving, to be lifted
By this selfish and unthinking effort.

ELOWYN  Ask me further, Hector, for I, know that

The man hath never shown any goodwill
Towards his brothers; so do not for a
Single moment believe he'll his promise
Keep and if he forgot not his agreement
The very second after he made it,
Turned his back and headed homeward
to his
Friend then will I deem thy chastisement
of
My request to him as entirely just.
(Enter Sergei.)

SERGEI     My lord, the prisoner hath now been
gaoled
And your presence needed at the palace.

HECTOR     I will be there soon. What news of the
field?

SERGEI     They say that Lord Anselm hath gone
missing,
And that Zaradrus safe remains behind
The defense of the imperial army.

HECTOR     What's that more are you are afraid to
tell us?

SERGEI     The news of my Lord Anaxarkos is
That I have more to tell and that he hath
Been badly injured and entirely brought

Down to the ground and that he is
grievous
Wounded and hath suffered a great loss
of
Blood and he hath from the field been
removed.

ELOWYN  And was he thus injured by whom,
Sergei?

SERGEI  'Twas Wesleyan that downed him, my
Lady.

ELOWYN  With that bit of information, Hector,
I will rest my case and consider thy
Unfair castigation of my deed nulled;
But wait thou for the full evil of my
First born to show its certain self to thee:
And with it all the horror of his birth
Will manifest to annihilate and
Justify my entreatment; rest assured.

## Act 3 Scene 4
## A deserted temple,
## At the edge of the Battlefield of Axainos

ELLIS     Thou hast brought me here with thee on
          thy work
          I thank ye, Malacus and yet from this
          Old temple where thou hast been
          stationed I
          Can only hear that busy field that doth
          Rage, and the sounds of metal doth reach
          From a far where I am not allowed so
          Tell me Malacus that there is more, but
          …

MALACUS  Move, boy

ELLIS               But Malacus I have the edge;
          Just think, I have the edge of the field
          when
          The real thing blusters in the middle that
          I have no access to; how goes it there?
          How does it feel to face the action real.

MALACUS    Move, boy, I have not finished my
          work yet .

ELLIS     And yet hearken thou the noise, the
          raging;
          Tell me why will ye not take me to it?

MALACUS     Art thou deaf and knowest thou not
the cost
Of disobedience in the battlefield
For which thou and I will pay with our
lives;
Now cease thou thy prattle and help me
to
Prepare the ground as they have us
ordered
For them to bring the injured king here to
Rest, away from the field; by this
temple's
Door prepare the ground for the king to
lie.

ELLIS     Is the king that severely injured then?

MALACUS     We are supposed to silence mouths of
words,
And speak instead with our hands at our
work.

ELLIS     But Malacus, he ain't dying, is he?

MALACUS     Rest, Ellis, he needs to rest, for he hath
Lost lot of blood, but once recovered will
Rejoin the battle, but here they come, my
Lord Dion and the soldiers all them
bringing
In the injured and much enfeebled king.

ELLIS      Gogs, I am here in defiance of his

Orders and therefore I must not be here

Seen by the king, You care for him. I'm gone.

(Exit Ellis. Enter, Dion, soldiers, Anaxarkos)

ANAXARKOS See I that my wounds doth bleed like the streams

Of Axainos, but feel not pain that is

So intense and so excruciating

That it doth attain its zenith where one

Doth transcends it to see but feels it not.

So Dion, my wounds and condition, both doth

Concern me not, but Anselm does and why

Have we not heard a thing from him for two

Past hours now with no news, no trumpet sounds,

No knowledge where and whom Wesleyan fights.

DION      It is not known.

ANAXARKOS          Perhaps then he is there

Where Anselm is, and fighting him right

now

And for all that we know near to killing
him

As he nearly did kill me and because

His chariot is too far away, we have

Had no news; for all we know he could
have

Maimed or even killed Anselm already.

DION         Herakles accompanies Anselm, brother
And thou knowest well that he will
guide him.

ANAXARKOS Not enough, Dion, not enough to
have my
Worries diminished, and therefore,  leave
thou
Me here to take the path that Anselm
took
This morning, seek him out and know of
him.

DION         Thou art yet weak and I canst leave thee
not
Unprotected, but hear, that the loud
noise
Was what, of what was it, soldier, what
goes?

ANAXARKOS Go thou follow it and leave me here

with
One guard at my attendance; leave at
once.

DION      This soldier will this entrance guard.
Shout out
Thy need of him if, when it doth occurs.
(Dion and soldiers leave. Enter Abdon)

ABDON     Anaxarkos, thou art fainted, wake up,
Anaxarkos, wake up, boy.

ANAXARKOS                        It's Abdon?

ABDON     Wake up Anaxarkos, and hear my words
My son, for thou hast cruel war to fight
And cannot give way to remorse or to
Weakness and never change for although
thou
Canst some respite earn with weakness
and thou
Canst thy strength regain with remorse
but soon
Thou wilst need to give these up;  get up
Despite thy fresh and bleeding wounds
and pain
And take thy beating straight back to the
war
To receive upon festers old, new wounds
Regardless of thy weakness and hurting.

Therefore, get thee up boy, Anaxarkos?

ANAXARKOS Abdon is; but I canst not see him
well.

ABDON    What is it that worries ye, my child as
Ye liest there thinking about the rights
And wrongs not unlike Amos that
wond'reth
Whether he should come or go and
thereby
In the process reacheth not anywhere,
But drops further into a quagmire of
Doubt and rhetoric, and freezes further
To inaction and immobility.
Anaxarkos, do thyself a favour:
Ask thyself, where doth thy
contemplation
Take thee; if this be time to think or act?

ANAXARKOS Grandsire, father, thou hast appeared
before
Me like an apparition and the sight
Of thee doth fills me with encouragement
Where otherwise I had crippling fear for
Anselm and before deathly remorse for
His son that weigheth down upon my
neck.
My legs are weakened by the folly of

My deed, my good grandsire speak thou
to me.

ABDON     Think not of Anselm for he is able
          And an adult warrior, but think thou
          more
          Of young Anius instead whom thou hast
          killed
          By your ineffectual thinking, thereby
          Think thou about thyself; look at thyself;
          Place thyself at the centre of your
          thoughts
          That thou art the problem and not the
          boy
          That is dead and not the father that is
          As able as a warrior can be that
          Fights under a weak and ineffectual
          Lead; you are your problem, Anaxarkos.
          Look at yourself, my son, lying here hurt
          And overcome by Wesleyan and think
          About why this is happening and why
          Thou art unable to better chief, and
          Why you are murdering your own
          people?

ANAXARKOS My heart paineth me.

ABDON                              Why?

ANAXARKOS                              Of Wesleyan.

ABDON     Tell me Anaxarkos how much dost thou
Really want to kill thy bent enemy
And how much do you want Aristos
dead
And, more important than anyone else,
How much do you want Wesleyan to
die?

ANAXARKOS Killing Wesleyan is my only aim.

ABDON     Not enough an aim that it doth make
thee
Retaliate with bloody blow for ev'ry
Single body blow of his, but only
Enough for to his unrelenting wounds
Receive, to run and to whimper away.

ANAXARKOS Wesleyan, I do not love but speak to
Me, my father, about Aristos, that
Should be the same to me as is Anselm,
Should he not, or must I forget that we
Are both descendents of the one
grandsire ?

ABDON     Again wadest thou into the waters
Of deep thought, but Anaxarkos as thou
Art at war now cease thy wayward
thinking
For while think you them cousins, act
they on

You as enemy; and while indulge you
Yourself in higher, godly aspects of
Your personality; act they upon
The base and animal aspect of theirs;
And while you think of the wastefulness
of
Spilling blood and think of saving lives,
they
Act upon the taking of your life and
Drawing of blood; because of one reason
And this one reason alone, that, they
doth
Consider not this an yearly season
Of druids practice to prove their theories
Of life and death, but they consider this
A war, the theatre of carnage, wherein
Hath slaughter, butchery, bloodshed,
Whereon
Only one god doth rule: the god of death.

ANAXARKOS Then sayest thou that man must not
retain
Redeeming humanity and become
Animal and thoughtless of recompense?

ABDON  Thou need'st not become what thou
already
Art, son: we are not descendent from the

Celestial heavens but art animals,
Born in a manner similar to the
Predators with the same taste for blood
as
Have they. Tell yourself that as a human
Being thou hast already done what thou
couldst
To prevent war, but now that all
attempts
By thee hath failed thou must allow thy
thirst
For blood, which thou possess'st innately
to
Take thee over, and therefore must thou
let the
Outlawed jungle law rule over thee now.

ANAXARKOS Pray father tell me what that law
dictates?

ABDON        The law of the jungle is the law of
Survival's end,  boy, a law sworn by
those
That hath not the wherewithal to indulge
In philosophy; states that either you
Live or your enemy lives, and that both
Cannot survive this war's hostilities;
The law states if you do not firstly kill

Thine enemy, who's Wesleyan, he'll kill
Thee instead; and will he kill all of you
One by one as he has with dead Anius
Begun, and now maybe next already
By now Anselm killed; we knoweth not
yet.

ANAXARKOS O but the Gods have upon me the
Mercy to forgive me for my change of
Mind for this mode of thinking doth
affect
Me to a state past argument for when
The land is on me placed can I for fear
Of recompense sacrifice dear lives of
Of all my bloody kin. He says I must
Kill mine enemy before they doth kill
Us whereby is question posed where is
there
Recompense if I earn it with the lives
Of mine own sparing the once removed
foe.

ABDON     Wesleyan's out there to kill you and he
Suffers no remorse nor doubt, and thus is
Able to torture thee to near dying.
Therefore see thou his deed, look thou at
thy
Bloody wounds, feel thou their pain, and

in them
Know, see, and feel thou Wesleyan's
hatred. (Abdon fades away. Enter
Malacus)

MALACUS    My Lord! I heard thee call.  Art thou
all right?

ANAXARKOS Where is he?

MALACUS                              Thou hath sleep; I
looked o'er thee.

ANAXARKOS A dream, then that is what it was;
here, lad
Hast thee the latest information yet?

MALACUS    I heard them say Lord Anselm hath
been found.
He is alive and well and fighting in
The far south-end of the field as last
heard.

ANAXARKOS Thou tells it well; give me thy hand,
my boy.

MALACUS    But mine firm orders from Lord Dion
are that
Thou art to be rested and not moved, yet.

ANAXARKOS I too can give thee orders, soldier,
now

What else is of the battle newly heard.

ANAXARKOS Nothing more was heard, my Lord for we art
Worried that although the sun is quite near
Setting yet whether Zaradrus is dead
Or not is yet unknown for no soldier
Here hath yet heard the happy trumpet sounds.
And no one knows we have yet won or lost.

ANAXARKOS Well then, we must go back and suss things out.

MALACUS    Are we to return to the camp, my lord?

ANAXARKOS Yes, boy, whither we with arms and steed we will
Reinforce, and then to return the fight.
(Exit Anaxarkos and Malacus)

## Act 3 Scene 5
### House of Hector, Axainos.

BILL     Tina. Hearest thou these happy made sounds: this trumpeting; that clamouring of clangs. For what happy cause are they making them.

TINA     To celebrate our victory, stupid. We've won the battle and the war, now here, have some sense and prepare for the party.

BILL     Art thou certain that we have won the war?

TINA     Art thou certain outside the sun hath set?

BILL     That it has, yes and that it doth does set every day upon the dreams of Billy and upon the happiness of the meagre and miserly cook.

TINA     This day, thou strutting cockerel, the sun hath set upon the sons of Ortellius.

BILL     O stupid me, what does that mean, I wonder?

TINA     The sons of Honorius have won and the war is over.

BILL     Praise be to each one of the Gods in

heaven. Long live Lord Aristos. The Sons of Honorius hath won. Long live Lord Aristos.

TINA     From whence this sudden loyalty for hast thou not strutted about feathers up on high saying that thou wast stood firmly on the fence.

BILL     O, I am very loyal now that the war is over, finished, in the past, history, and the hostilities won by whom, Lord Aristos be it, then say I "Long live Bill the baker", or perchance it be won by Lord Anaxarkos then also say I "Long live Bill the baker" for if the war was won by Lord Dubs the donkey even then, bray I "Long live Billy." "Long live Billy" "Long live Billy"

TINA     Well, now how fickle is that, unlike me who prays nightly for the happiness of my King, Aristos, and all my life says only, "Long live King Aristos."
(Enter Elowyn.)

ELOWYN     What noise is here and had I not said that There should be total silence in this room?

TINA    Canst we not celebrate or canst ye not see
        that the sun has set, and thy son has not
        yet Zaradrus killed. Ye cannot us order
        around no more for we have won for
        ever and thou hast forever lost.
        (Enter Hector. Exit the servants.)

HECTOR  Sister, no definite information
        Of the results on the battlefield to
        Our confused ear hath reached us yet;
        stay calm.

ELOWYN  I trust my sons completely, Hector, yes,
        Although, I can see that the sun hath set
        As they do so triumphantly proclaim,
        I choose to unsee it for the knowledge
        In my heart doth tells me it's yet over,
        That my sons are still alive, and that my
        Anselm hath not lost in this manner
        tame.

HECTOR  Celebrations are as yet contained just
        To the streets while the palace still awaits
        For information, but I am with thee
        In the belief that this war cannot end
        Without some effort from us all and so
        Let me tell thee of the last report from
        The field wherein was that Anaxarkos
        Is now the roaring success in the war

And this before the setting of the sun

ELOWYN  Well I am extremely happy to hear
Of this; where before I had told thee that
Fighting will sooner or later become
Him and in a matter of time would his
Behaviour change; it pleases me to know
He now fights as ere him his father did.

HECTOR  Well, Elowyn, in this manner people
Change and this the manner war
survives, but,
I have other news that will please thee or
Not, I cannot tell: this morning, it was
Well heard Wesleyan spared the life of
Dion.

ELOWYN  What? "Wesleyan spared the life of
Dion?" And
What dost thou mean when thou
speakest those words?
Speak thou in details or speak not at all.

HECTOR  Details, well, the details are that when
Wesleyan and Dion fought a battle harsh,
Wesleyan did defeat Dion and that quite
Completely, and yet he did not kill him?

ELOWYN  "Did not kill him?" And these words
meaneth what?

HECTOR    How difficult is it to understand
That Dion was defeated upon the ground
By Wesleyan, but instead of stabbing
Him dead, he touched with the arm of
his bow
The fallen arm of Dion, and insulted
Dion
With words like eunuch and ignorant
fool,
And then he spared his life, let him go as
By the Pontus he had promised to do.

ELOWYN    Fallen down and defenseless if Dion was
He would be naturally spared, for it
Is against the rules to kill a man down.

HECTOR    But this case wherein one did the other
Overcome and if every enemy
Is not downed; and quite defenseless
before
The fatal stroke, honestly, Elowyn.

ELOWYN    Then, there must exist some other
motive.

HECTOR    Let it go now for my question is that
If this incident indicates the chance
That Wesleyan is keeping his promise
To you then, pray, I wish to know thy
thoughts.

ELOWYN  My thoughts? Make thy question more
specific.

HECTOR  Well, then, all right, if Wesleyan adheres
To the promise to thee given and he
Spares the lives of Anaxarkos and of
Dion, will you then reveal his truth and
his
Real identity to his brothers three?

ELOWYN  When you ask, "Will I reveal Wesleyan's
Identity", what you ask of me is
"Will I end this war?"

HECTOR                               Why, yes, certainly
The revelation will lead to the quick
Cessation of hostilities for sure.


ELOWYN Not without certainty of Wesleyan's
Allegiance to Anaxarkos will I
Do anything such disastrous deed,
Hector.

HECTOR  If he spared their lives, he is allegiant.

ELOWYN  Hector, what I cannot see is that he
Hath left the side of Aristos and or that
He hath ceased fighting for Aristos'
cause

HECTOR  He still is with Aristos, I agree.

ELOWYN    Then the change in his attitude is not
          Proven by this false battle with Dion, when
          Earlier, he all but killed Anaxarkos
          And wounded him so badly that he was
          Forced off the field. Who almost kill my son,
          Hector, that same Wesleyan who today
          Hath pretended to keep his word to me.

HECTOR    You will do nothing to end this war, then?

ELOWYN    Other than watch as the boy struts about
          On his pride around the empty  promise
          That he, like the comical but dang'rous
          Clown, made to me, what I can and will do
          Is watch tomorrow's Wesleyan afield,
          Which will again prove to thee that he is
          And doth remains enemy to my sons.

HECTOR    And if his actions tomorrow doth prove
          Otherwise to spare the lives of the three,
          What then?
          (The sun is seen in the sky)

ELOWYN               Hector, do look outside upon
          The sight most odd and amazing of the
          Sun whereof earlier hath we witnessed

its
Setting to encase whole world in dark
But now still there low in the sky, but
large
And red above the Axainian Hilltops
Is already set sun seen yet again.
What is the reason for this whimsical
Demeanour of the now set, now 'risen
Sun that we are strangely now
witnessing?

HECTOR    And hear thou also the cessation of
The sounds of revelries in the street.
Guard!
(Enter guard.)

HECTOR    What has it in the streets? What's going
on?

GUARD    My Lord, the behaviour of the sun hath
Puzzled all, whereof the first said that the
Sun had set and Zaradrus was alive
And so the people celebrated; but,
Now they say the sun is seen once more
and
Zaradrus is dead; stop celebrating.

HECTOR    I will to the palace now to find out
What hath transpired and then send thee
word.

## Act 3 Scene 6

### Anaxarkos' Camp, Axainos.

(Malacus and the others enter carrying
the body of Ellis)

PREFECT  Is that the errant boy Ellis that was
Ordered not to afield to join the fight?

MALACUS   He was struck, beside  some that
accompanied
Him, that say this body is his, but I
Canst tell not for it is grievously hit,
And so bloodied is he in the face I
Canst recognise it not, but if he is
Ellis the boy then not with me does the
Fault of his death lie for although thou
didst
Say that he should follow orders of the
King, it was the dead boy's fault that he
did
Disobey.

PREFECT                          Uncover his body. Yes,
It is him. Soldiers, have it disappeared
That the information of his death be
Retained from the king who now being
around
Too much to do can be informed of it
Later when not confronted by the news

Of the state; hurry; before he arrives.

(Sounds of celebration. Enter Anaxarkos)

ANAXARKOS Yes, man. How goes it?

PREFECT                              Regarding the sun,

Your highness we hath naught but

turmoil with

Trumpets on, then off, and now on again.

ANAXARKOS Well, defeat is not near us yet, that's

for

Certain, and the battle not yet at their

Side and even though I have noticed that

We have lost the boy, yet his matter must

Survive for the days when we are in

power.

PREFECT  Disobedience the sin of a soldier

Put his Nan to the dire fate she hath

feared.

(Exit soldiers. Enter Dion)

DION       Brother, Anaxarkos, I entreat thee

To kill me, so that  after this, thou lets

Me live no more as my life is now the

Carrion dead that has not in it the stuff

Of survival for in letting me live

Did the Charioteer's son kill me outright

And now am I naught but dead though

living.

ANAXARKOS For what reason are these words of
   defeat,
   Dion; distressed words that make thy
   countenance
   So dark that they doth eclipse thy spirit
   To dark quite completely and entirely?

DION   What words should my defeated tongue
   speak then?

ANAXARKOS Words of anger that hath in them the
   power
   To shake away the night by bringing
   back
   The moon; speak radiant Dion I know
   and love.

DION   Maybe that Dion died when the
   whoreson
   His weapon perked over and above mine
   Head when instead of springing to my
   feet
   Back to strike in retaliation did
   I limply lie in helplessness looking
   At his angry face beyond his pointing
   Sword unable to think or act or fight.

ANAXARKOS Are those the sounds of Anselm's

chariot heard?

(Enter the Herakles)

HERAKLES   Good cheer and shout "huzza"
         Anaxarkos,
         For good victory is in our hand that
         Carryeth high on our shoulders the red
         Beacon of the killing of Zaradrus.

ANAXARKOS Happiness indeed; felicitations
         To ye that must now tell the entire camp
         How that giant hand did toy with the
         sun.

 HERAKLES Let Anselm himself tell you of it, for
         Here the prince comes victorious in his
         vow.
         (Enter Anselm)

ANAXARKOS What happy words hast thou for us,
         brother?

ANSELM   Sweetened with revenge, Sir, and
         dripping with
         Honeyed success of the lost battle won.

ANAXARKOS Some more of that for us to revel in.

ANSELM   Well then hear the story for thou
         knowest
         That impregnable was their defense
         around

Zaradrus, making our get-past unsure,
That kept us at bay the entire day in
Growing frustration and to no success,
More to no avail. Then in the evening
Did Herakles and I decide to forge way
To win through trick and strategy being
our
Only recourse else would the war be lost.
And this was our trick that Herakles did
make
The horse hooved dust of past days upon
the
Plains to rise by invoking the wind wild
That rolled with such intensity that it
Did bedust the entire twilight sky at
The far end of the field to make it seem
As though the sun, which was obscured,
hath set,
And the night and darkness was bought
in
And the day hath ended with Zaradrus
Alive: seemed to as though they hath
won.

ANAXARKOS Thou caused the dust to rise and
shield'th the sun?
But that is quite stupendous in its
thought?

HERAKLES   Yet with the soldier's feet it can be
          done.

ANAXARKOS Didst thou always know?

ANSELM                        Maybe we did, but
          They did not and Zaradrus proud and
          now
          Fearless in his victory came out from
          Behind their impenetrable defense,
          In plain sight and for me to raise my
          bow,
          Strike him unto the ground to deserving
          death.

ANAXARKOS Ho, Anselm aren't thou quite the
          villain then.

ANSELM   And presently the dust did settle, and
          The sun was revealed, to show once
          more as
          Before a late evening signaled by the
          Horizon's low red heavy sun quite near
          To setting yet still in the sky shining
          Over the body of slain Zaradrus
          That lay in the dust where I had shot him
          As per my vow, and then above the hills
          Of Axainos the sun did really set
          But not before I had avenged my son.

ANAXARKOS That is one battle safely behind us.

HERAKLES  I ask why Dion receives us not nor us
      Congratulates with naught, but his
      silence.
      Wesleyan's attack got his tongue as well?

DION    He caught me at a sad time when hath
      my
      Confidence deserted me, that is all.

ANAXARKOS No, Herakles, it is a matter far
      Serious than he dismisses it to naught.
      The one there hath caused Dion and me
      both be
      Grievously wounded and then hath let
      us
      Go like some benevolent bequeather
      Of our lives, or is he playing with us?
      Rather than sulk at his treatment of us
      We must now plan his death and that is
      now
      Our one and single most important task.

DION    Plan, Herakles, plan, let us plan, for it
      Would mean that I was benign with him
      only
      Because I wanted to delay my sure
      Retaliation that was to be him
      Bequeathed in form of a plan and, it

Would mean that I let him go free only
Momentarily; and therefore, my friend,
Let us sit down to chart his final path,
Through the forests of our weapons and
the
Death knolls of our strikes; let us hack
out a
Path and make his unerring road to
death

ANAXARKOS Herakles, think thou for it must be
done.

HERAKLES    Well, yes, we have an hour or so to
rest,
But time enough for us to plan our strike
Against, yes, Wesleyan that is more than
Ever dangerous to us now; be cheered.

## Act 4

### The Battlefield

CHORUS    And so that night, the events were at
                    such
                    A high and the time was so delayed that
                    The armies returned not to camp to rest
                    And recover as the custom was, instead
                    Remained upon the battlefield itself
                    To avert a day's delay and waited
                    For the sun to rise upon the next day,
                    The fourteenth day of war; the while on
                    one
                    Side of the field by torch light did the
                    sons
                    Of Ortellius chart out their battle plan.

                    Herakles said they could kill Wesleyan
                    Only if he was weakened first and so,
                    Their entire focus should rest upon how
                    To divest him of the deadly and lethal
                    Dart of Ilmarinen that was his strength.
                    The dart of Ilmarinen, the weapon
                    That did make Wesleyan invincible
                    Against Anselm, was made specially for
                    The warrior by the celestial blacksmith
                    Exclusively with Anselm's death in mind
                    Its power was surefire and its use,

Though singular in that it could not be
Twice used was lethal in that it never
Missed its mark. The one and only time that
Wesleyan used it, Anselm's death was
ensured.
By the flickering torch lights on the field,
The Sons of Ortellius decided that
The only way to divest Wesleyan
Of this dart was to force him to use it
In the battle that day 'gainst someone else
Other than Anselm and the question was
Who would sacrifice his life for this cause?
Here, it was Dion that said he would like to
Volunteer the name of a warrior brave
That considered his life's aim to settle
Previous scores with Wesleyan and had asked
For the honour of combating with him,
And if anyone could do the needful,
It was his brave and strong Typhus that could.
Typhus, son of Dion was enormous,
Thick of the neck, lumbering, fearless and whose

Very presence did invoke great terror
Amongst the ordinary soldiers on
Whom he used this fact to his advantage
To become the undefeated opponent
That he was known to be. Hopeful of a
Victory, the Ortellii, did therefore
Agree on Typhus to lead the attack.
And thus, while it was still dark, but daylight
Approaching, the sound of  bugles signaled
Recommencement of the battle when the
Trembling light of torches shewed that Typhus
Walked slow and sure towards the enemy.
The sounds of his footsteps echoed lumb'rous
And loud, and hearing him advance darkly
The soldiers felt the  turbulence in the
Air caused by his amplitude and saw that
By intermittent gusts the torches were
Snuffed out and the terrified field was in
Black darkness shrouded until lights were relit.
Typhus' target, Wesleyan stood steady
And unafraid for he knew that his foe did

His faculty of creating fear use as a
Weapon and the only way to counter
Fear was control; and thus the fight
began.
Typhus invoked a chimera that would
Have most mortals terrified, but calmly
Did Wesleyan destroy by invoking
A counter to his illusion, whereat
Typhus created more apparitions
All of which with sheer calm and skill
were by
Wesleyan destroyed, when Typhus then
did
Retaliate by slaying of Wesleyan's
Horses and bringing his chariot down
then
Charging against him, but by then had his
foe,
Wesleyan climbed quickly on another
Steed to the fight resume and with that
was
Typhus at loss as to what next to do.
He had to think quite differently, for if
Wesleyan was proving impossible
To unnerve, then he needed opponents
That would be easily frightened, that's
when

Typhus remembered the clout he hath
had
On Aristos' army at the time that
He had first advanced upon it when he
Had caused them all to retreat in fear and
Terror, and had smelt success in the air.
So, it was towards the army the
Daemon his attention turned, and like
one
Possessed attacked the soldiers and
complete
Chaos created to design their sure
Destruction and his certain victory.
Without fine knowledge of weaponry, the
Ordinary soldiers were quite useless
Against Typhus and were many, many
Thousands slaughtered, and great rivers
of blood
Flowed upon the plains and wave of
terror
Spread amongst the troops fleeing in
panic
To turmoil and chaos ev'rywhere; then
Was Wesleyan at a loss for he hath
Planned to weaken and to kill Typhus
with
Ordinary weapons, but now with the

Army being attacked and the destruction
Of the entire army in certain sight,
He had to then think another way out.
Another way there was one but wherein
To strike the daemon with the poisoned
dart
Of Ilmarinen, which Wesleyan hath
As a surety against Anselm and
Which if now used uselessly on Typhus,
The lesser foe would Wesleyan weaken
In the war against Anselm; and yet if
Typhus won this battle and destroyed the
Entire army, the war itself would end.
Therefore Wesleyan, did decide to save
The war and took the only course he had
To shoot at Typhus his adored weapon
His strength and the surety of his success.
The son of Dion saw the blaze and the
trail
Of the blazing dart on fire as it did
Approach him, and the giant began to in
Fear retreat, as fierce winds began to
blow,
Loud thunder sound to announce
approaching
Star of death that heavens rent asunder
With its fiery trail to its target find,

Whom it pierced right through his
beating heart and
Typhus, the son of Dion then mortally
Injured did fall down deprived of his life.
With this, that battle ended in the hours
Of the fifteenth morning when Wesleyan
Hath the war, but lost the dart and was he
Greatly weakened, and in the détente that
Ensued did Anaxarkos' army that
Hath success but lost their son did mourn
the
Death of Typhus. Early high was the sun
Upon the sky when retreat and rest was
Out of question and the soldiers rested
Quite tiredly, and with eyes deprived of
Sleep then picked their weapons to
resume the
Fight that morn of the fifteenth day of
war.

## Act 4 Scene 1
### House of Hector

HECTOR   In our days with the limits of war kept
In sight always were the rules never
crossed
Which now are broken in a manner thus
To give the soldiers no rest, increase their
Desperation, decrease their endurance
Resulting then in hastening of this sad
Carnage, this senseless, ceaseless
slaughter of
Humanity. How many incessant
Days more of this whereto must we
fatigued
Stand as mute witness: our tormented
thought
Hath been this all of today. That times
change
I understand but why does life always
Remain unseeingly in stasis when
The days are raging utmost at their
worst?

ELOWYN   They, the sons of Honorius, hath brought
this
Into proud being and when a forgiving
chance

Was given to them to end it in peace
They did take it not. It is not as though
They were denied the chance to accept
peace.

HECTOR  And so will this state be ended only
By complete annihilation for towards
This destructive end hath once the staid
and
Wise people that hath firm belief in life's
Preservation not just Anaxarkos
But all those like him are now entirely
changed
To norm of obliterating violence
And the bloody moral of blood for blood.

ELOWYN  When have I ever said that we should all
Be thirsty for blood, but yes, my appeal
Hath been to hunger for justice and
rights;
And why should this injustice done to us
Not affect poor Anaxarkos alone,
When he is after all his father's son
And born to traverse in his kingly path?

HECTOR  Yes, why should it not, but yesterday in
Repetition again did the life of
Dion, Wesleyan spare or dost thou wish
not

To comment upon its occurrence just yet?

ELOWYN  Or do I wish to make a  comment that
This same Wesleyan earlier left no
Stone unturned to ensure his victory
Against poor Typhus the son of Dion
And staked his everything to the battle
Save and with it to save his future chance
To kill my sons, and here I say to thee
The need for fair comment on Wesleyan's
Actions against Typhus doth not rest
with
Me alone.

HECTOR                           Keeping aside for the
time
Being, Wesleyan's battle against Typhus,
What dost thou think of this next sparing
Dion?

ELOWYN  Well, Hector thou dost this day heckle
me,
For thou also hast the report read that
Said Wesleyan struck Dion first when
did
Roughly ride after him, rudely called him
Unto the battle, and ruthlessly him
Attacked, and only then let go; not once,
But many a haughty time and each time

Did he likewise, to provoke Dion, and to

Torture him and then leave him; pray, do

tell

Me in what part of those words betwixt

lines

Didst thou read that he did this deed out

of

Brotherly love?

HECTOR                          And yet, Elowyn, both

Times that he did attack Dion he let him

Go; not once, but twice he did spare his

life.

Is he not trying to tell thee something?

ELOWYN  Or is he pretending to keep his word

To me so I can fortuitously

End this war, cease hostilities, and give

The throne of Axainos to him my first

Born for him then gift it free of cost to

Aristos; and this done when my sons are

Not yet dead, but left with ragged

nothing

To live on wretched and misbegotten

Like lost souls that would have been

better off

Dead. Well then Hector, I do implore

thee

To thy vision widen and to see in
Wesleyan's manner, pride and insolence
And to not see in it,  with a stretch of
The imagination, humility,
Repentance or remorse; and furthermore
Hector, wait for Anaxarkos newly
Changed that will the errant give his
desert.

HECTOR    I will wait for it, but sister, if he doth
Mystifyingly hastens my point by
Sparing once more Anaxarkos' life as
He did Dion twice before, then what
wilst thou?

ELOWYN    I will wait for what is yet to be, if
And when that ever happens, we shall
see.

## Act 4 Scene 2
### The battle field of Axainos

CYPRUS    Anaxarkos. Where is he? Is he here?
Anaxarkos. Call the man thither, now.
(Enter Dion, Herakles)

HERAKLES    Dion, hearest thou the voice of
Cyprus?
He will here asking for Anaxarkos.
Send the word out for him and tell him to
Come hither at once from where he
maybe.

DION    Is the master here?

CYPRUS    (voice)                    Anaxarkos. Get
Me Anaxarkos.

HERAKLES                    Urgently, go Dion
And waste no time to Anaxarkos find
And bring here.

DION                    He is just in from the north.
(Exit Dion.)

CYPRUS (voice) Anaxarkos!
(Enter Anselm.)

HERAKLES                    Anselm. The voice of the
Master doth rent the air with urgency
And torture and they all are much afraid.

ANSELM   But, my man, knowest thou what has
         happened;
         When battle was raging at its heights,
         Hath the master suddenly called fighting
         Off and asked for Anaxarkos, but why?

HERAKLES   I am told that Anaxarkos is found
         By Dion and now will he here to tend to
         The master lost, abandoned by his son.

ANSELM   Abandoned by Leroy, but how dost
         thou?
         Hark, again.

CYPRUS                   Anaxarkos, where art thou?
         (Enter Dion and Anaxarkos)

ANAXARKOS But what hath occurred and what be
         it here?

HERAKLES   The news hath been conveyed to
         Cyprus that
         His son Leroy's dead.

ANAXARKOS                   But the dead still lives
         And Leroy by me far north hath been
         seen.

DION     Yes, but he knoweth not and now all
         rests
         On ye, brother for the master doth stand
         Like an immovable obstacle 'fore

Us and the only way we can proceed
To victory is by removing him:
Either by trick or by a strategy.

ANSELM  What? Make him stop by telling him a
lie?

DION  Yes, but the master doth suspect that it
Is a lie for it was his stricture that
Did teach us if the war could not be won
By means fair then by all means do use
foul.

ANSELM  He taught us that to use foul means was
one
Recourse available, and certainly -
Certainly not the proper way for us.

DION  Anyway, although we have lied, the man
Believes it is a lie and therefore doth
He ask for you that hath yet ne'er spoken
Falsehood until now, to tell him the
truth,
And needs must that thou shouldst lie
for us by
Telling him as have we that his son's
dead.

ANSELM  Anaxarkos, let us not lie for to
Fight with lie as weapon is coward's

way.

DION      Anslem, fighting with weapons is useless
             Against one such as the master that hath
             Taught us the the very use of weapons and
             That knoweth our every weakness and strength;
             And who is so high of the mind that we
             Canst not the higher climb therefore, let us
             To overcome him debase ourselves, let's
             Do whatever it takes to take him out.

HERAKLES   Whether you want to lie or speak the truth,
             The choice is yours for you to now decide.

DION      Here he cometh to put our victory
             Unto your hands, remember, brother, this
             The master is that doth block our path to
             Kill Wesleyan and if thou art righteous
             Now thou dost invite nought, but more
             death from him. (Enter Cyprus)

CYPRUS   Anaxarkos! Anaxarkos? Here mine
             Anaxarkos! Thou wilst tell me the truth.
             They say my son, my son, my beloved

Leroy hath been killed, and I looked for him
All over, but have found him not, yet it
Prays upon my mind whether they doth trick
Me to have me lay mine arms, or they doth
Speak the truth, and only thou, that never
Lies, can tell me what hath transpired, and thy
Pronouncement will be unquestioned by my
Belief in thy word; tell me is he dead?
(Anaxarkos silent)

CYPRUS      Thou speakest not and thou canst not lie and
Therefore thy silence doth indicateth that
They hath lied to overcome and kill me.

DION        Anaxarkos doth remains silent from
Grief, Master Cyprus for thy son, Leroy
Did bravely fight before was overcome
By our army and killed in the far north
Field where his last remains doth lifeless lie.

CYPRUS      I care not to lay my eyes upon him

Dead, which if proved, then this life is for
me
Over for how could the will to avenge
His death be mine when along with him I
Too hath ceased to live and one that is
dead
Hath no desires for revenge, nor war,
But, then think I do it cannot be that
A mere collection of soldiers can the
Son of Cyprus overcome that hath been
In combat instructed and skilled by the
Best and with the best of Princes, but do;
Anaxarkos let me hear from you if
He is really dead? Open your mouth and
Speak, son. Hath my reason for living
now
Departed from this firmament and life?

(Anaxarkos silent)

CYPRUS   That is it.  You all lie. Anaxarkos
Is unspeaking and take I my arms up
Again to fight the way a battle is
To be fought with arms and weapons if
thou
Art true, and with lies if thou art the
false.
Thus have I my arms taken up again

To take you to certain defeat and death.

ANAXARKOS No, master. No. But please, hear me
out.

CYPRUS Speak Anaxarkos speak for thou that
lives
Art like my son they say is dead, speak
now
I beseech ye, Anaxarkos, speak thou.

ANAXARKOS My master.

CYPRUS	Speak Anaxarkos!

ANAXARKOS	Leroy
Is dead, Master, thy son no longer lives.

CYPRUS No! No! Lie, Anaxarkos, the lie that
Doth prevents lacerations to the soul,
And soothes the burning with its falsing
balm,
That lie I wanted not, but wanted I
The truth of whether my boy be live or
Dead and I was given what I wanted.
I should have been careful for that I
asked
And got when I could have had the
other,
The lie, the pleasing wonderous lie that
my

Boy, my little boy is not yet dead but,
Lives. Instead, but now, I ask for strength to
Help me bear this terrifying truth that
Hath me killed in all but name to my life
Take unto its end for there is no more
Life for me without my son. The grief of
This hath me destroyed that it doth weaken
Me so much that I cannot even move.
The light in the sky shineth with brightness
And a brilliance that indicates it now
Is time for me to lay mine arms down and
To prepare for my death, and so in all
Obedience of heavenly light I kneel
In prayer to spend the final hours that did
End when my son's life hath ended, and for
My deeds that this kind of death did warrant
I do forgiveness and repentance seek.
(Enter Asahel the convict.)

DION      Asahel, the convict's here, Asahel,
Asahel, kill him now this be thy chance.

ANSELM  No, Asahel, he hath laid down his arms
And that is not right to strike him right at
This moment when he sits in prayer, which wilst
Makest repentence of his deed's
consequence.

Asahel:  Release me, Anselm, for so were my men
At prayer when this man them killed over a
Petty dispute to deem me convict and
Imprison me, but now this moment of
Revenge is mine and I will kill him not
Bearing in mind his position at prayer,
And caring not  for my deed's
consequence.

ANSELM  I warn thee Asahel, wield thy weapon
Not when the master is unarmed and
down.

Asahel:  Out my way Anselm, I know what to do.


(Asahel kills Cyprus)

## Act 4 Scene 3

**Outside the house of Hector.**

**Axainos**

        (Enter Tony and Tina)

TINA         Where is Billy?

TOM         Why?

TINA         The sure and surly guard is come.

TOM         To take the Bill away?

TINA         Either for that or because the crowd now gathered in the market square to protest the dastardly deed of Anaxarkos comes this way towards us and it may turn violent.

        (Enter Bill dressed as a girl.)

BILL         Crowds, I care not for crowds, but call you this murder flour, and what muddy bread must I bake with what looks as though it hath been milled from bones in the battlefield. Oh my! Look! A guard comes! Let us all speak of something else. Otherwise we will be ta'en.

        (Enter the guard.)

BILL         That vile and obnoxious man, Anaxarkos, that killed the good and the kind Master Cyprus, and what dishonourable falsehood was spake in the battle by them today to say that the still alive Leroy was indeed still and dead; oh fie upon them that shoot the darts of cowardice at their enemies, and strike their heads with the spears of deceit, and keep in their arsenal dishonest weapons of the weak; why, sir, how be ye, is everything well with your loved ones, how nice, well I would friends with ye, but I must be off for my dough turns sour with my not having tended it.

GUARD    Stay.

TINA    Are you, the guard, here to meet the master for there is a crowd gathered by the palace gates, we hear?

TOM    Yes, and it doth roar, but let me go see what it is about.
(Exit Tom)

TINA    They are protesting this heinous crime by the sorry sons of Ortellius, and why should they not? Come let us all to the palace gates and protest in one voice with the people.

BILL  Yes, come, let us protest.

GUARD Not you, here you, are you Bill, the baker of this house?

BILL  No, no, Bill is a man, silly and is there somewhere within the house baking his bread in some oven to the other for canst thou not feel the heat of its fire right here though we be so far away.

GUARD Who art thou, then?

BILL  I, his sister am.

GUARD To the field, Bill the baker.

BILL  But, women are not supposed to the field.

GUARD Cockle shells to pass off as breasts.

BILL  Oh…you! Oh, so you call me small; well I will have thee know, Mr. Biggles that I am considered, in fact, so considerable that I need these supports to give me a lift now and then and were I not a respectable sister of a respectable baker in a respectable household, I would show thee what problems large women have hidden in their enclosed emparts, but you strong men have nothing, but the

war and the battle field in mind, and
further more as thou wantest my brother
the baker, allow me to go find him for
you. Oh. Oh. No. Thou dost rape me,
lout.

GUARD    Your stuffing was not enough, come on,
Bill the baker.

BILL    No, but, first I have to ask permission
from the Lord, but he drags me away,
but help me, save me.
(Bill and guards exit. Enter Tom)

TOM    What a noise cometh this way. Can you
hear it? They see that it is come and
violent towards the house of Hector, and
that they are shouting, screaming,
throwing stones, and demanding of the
mother of the lying warrior to be handed
over to them.

TINA    The lying warrior hath a teeming mother
that hath ta'en my Billy away and her
death will be my revenge.

TOM    Where is hid thy knife?

TINA    In the dungeons, my pretty pipe, in the
form of the locked up, mad man Barobus,
for look at what have I here: it is the key

to his release and if we free him from his prison he will free her from her life; that is what I want, but that for later, for now the crowd wants the woman, oh and is her life severely wanted by all, but it also endangers us in her service so safest be it to lock ourselves in until the crowd has dispersed, then I will downstairs to do my bloody deed.

(They go in)

## Act 4 Scene 4
## On the battlefield

ARISTOS  King Hadrus of Ibrahimya, know that
Thy disorderly conduct suits not thee,
An indispensible ally and a
Premier friend of the imperial forces
That thou canst in this manner let go thy
Position when the war doth rages, and
Impel thou me to likewise, leave my
place.

HADRUS  To call you safe aside, my lord, was my
Only recourse thinking that you may
have
Appointed me my new position under
Rude compulsions of the plebian force
and
From thence you may be better able to
Reconsider your rashly decision.

ARISTOS  The battle doth rageth, Hadrus, that
leaves
No place for an indulgent, leisurely
Exchange of words. What's thy problem?
Quick thou.

HADRUS  Forgive me, Lord, but these that are but
mere
Wasteful utterances of the mouth for

Thee, for me are the gems and jewels on
My small throne of Ibrahimya in the
Imminent danger of being lost as are
My worthless wordy words and what for
thee
Is waste of time, for me is petition
To save a King from under the knave's
wheels .

ARISTOS    But thy new appointment hath no reason
To thee cause proud unhappiness, but
must
Be by thee with equanimity ta'en.

HADRUS    Long are our kingdoms affiliated,
But, Son of Honorius, forget not the
Heights of the Ibrahimii, which thou hath
Reduced by turning their ruler to drive
And placing their status lower than the
Wheels that he is being expected to drive.

ARISTOS    Forget not, father that after the death
Of Cyprus, Wesleyan is now reached the
Position of the forces' new command.

HADRUS    Well-appointed he may be, but that doth
Change not his birth at the loins of the
dam
Of the turner of the mire and its dirt.

ARISTOS   By that same argument, sire your being
          now
          Appointed his charioteer, changeth not
          Your birth amongst high sitters of golden
          Thrones, but no more of this talk, what
          other
          Argument hast thou, other than his
          birth?

HADRUS    His allegiance, my Lord, is entirely
          In question and is doubted by the host.

ARISTOS   His allegiance is with me, Ibrahimya.

HADRUS    Wesleyan is not to be trusted, sir.

ARISTOS   Are you yet wasting my time, King
          Hadrus?

HADRUS    I know and have observed, as have us all,
          The battles two wherein he did fight
          Dion,
          And whereof he could have easily killed
          Him, not once but twice, and this
          conduct of
          His remaineth quite unquestioned by
          thee.

ARISTOS   We spoke to him to his explanations
          Regarding those battles are by us got.

HADRUS    Oh, but must we hear of it and what are

> They, the explanations of him having
> Let go the two prime enemy alive?

ARISTOS   I have neither cause nor the time to tell
You, but let it suffice to say that he
Doth remains most allegiant to our cause.

HADRUS   In all honesty, do confess to me
Aristos, his behaviour troubles you.

ARISTOS   The perplexed men that he hath let go are
Minor and inconsiderable warriors,
Ibrahimya, for it is the one and
Yet uncontested and too contented
Anselm that is the danger true to our
Security and to our victory,
And regarding him I know that
Wesleyan's
Unwavering allegiance thereof rests
Upon my side; and with that assurance
King Hadrus, I command thee to return
To the fighting and to thy appointment.

HADRUS   Return to fighting, I will my lord, but
I will not become the driver of his
Tricky wheels that's not becoming of me.

ARISTOS   Lord Hadrus, I command to thee to thy
Appointment consider as similar
To that of Herakles who despite being

Of descent than thy ascendency is
Higher still the chariot of Anselm drives.

HADRUS That being the case then I will return
quite
Afeared to my worrisome appointment,
But have you know that we, Ibrahimyii
Have our ways and to serve the lineage
of
The wicker baskets is not what we were
Born to do; with that complaint, dear my
Lord,
I return in vain to the fight for ye.

## Act 4 Scene 5

### Inside the house of Hector, Axainos

(Noise of the mob.)

HECTOR Guard! What new situation is outside?

TOM The crowd is at the gate and the custody
of the Mistress their demand.

HECTOR Have the palace guards we called arrived
yet?

TOM A few guards only just arrived, my lord.


(Enter Elowyn)

HECTOR The doors of the house are strong and
can't be broken. They can't come in. Keep
guard outside


(Exit Tom)

ELOWYN It looks as though the battlefield hath to
This city and my house been extended.

HECTOR The battlefield, Elowyn, but had you
Been with me when I this morning went
there
Twice is as angry as is here this noise,
And the roar that's heard outside is not
half
As bad as that we saw out on the field.

ELOWYN The battle field is filled with slush I
      heard.

HECTOR Blood, worthless, unnecessarily spilt
      From the senseless bodies that day felled
      to
      Mercilessly be left there rotting 'cause
      No one was from the inescapable
      Affray freed to clear the littered heads,
      and
      Feet, and arms, and torsos; and then was
      there
      The difficulty of the soldiers that
      Slipped and slid upon blood and gore
      and
      Yet faught on.

ELOWYN        I am not afraid, Hector.

HECTOR Be very afraid Elowyn, for it hath
      happened.
      Didst thou hear?

ELOWYN       What's this crowd?

HECTOR Not the crowd, I speak not of this paltry
      Crowd but of war and of Wesleyan that
      Hath, didst thou not hear, committed the
      act
      Whereof I was certain that he would

soon
And thou averred that he would never
do.

ELOWYN   Yes, Hector, I heard of it but do tell.

HECTOR   Wesleyan spared Anaxarkos' again.
(The noise of the crowd increases. Enter
Tom)

TOM      My Lord the people break the gates
outside.

HECTOR   Are not palace guards yet controlling
them?

TOM      Only three guards here, my Lord, and
there, a people almost a hundred.

HECTOR   Fasten the doors and casements, that may
let us hear ourselves over and 'bove the
noise.

ELOWYN   Yes, Hector, I heard that Wesleyan did
Spare the life of Anaxarkos, the news,
Which shall be verified by Sergei that
I can see arrived at the gate from here.

TOM      My Lord, Sergei is unable to get past the
crowd with message he doth carry.

HECTOR   Bring him in from the entrance at the
back.

(Enter Sergei.)

ELOWYN  Yes, speak Sergei. we all awaiteth thee.

SERGEI  Wesleyan and Anaxarkos hath both
A bloody battle fought, I bring to thee.

HECTOR  Of battle is thy news and not of death?

SERGEI  No death, my lord, but of the fight that was
Bloody, heartless and quite terrifying.

ELOWYN  Tell us of it, then.

SERGEI                              My lady, battle
Fair of arms and argent it was not, but
Torture and distress passed of as a war.

ELOWYN  Sergei, the final account of a war
Adds up to wins and losses, wherein is
Fair mindedness cancelled and whereacross
Is justice carried over, yet speak on.

SERGEI  The battle, my lady, did proceed thus:
Thrice was Anaxarkos called to fight by
Wesleyan and thrice my Lord did answer
His call whereat each time did Wesleyan
Him pursue and overcome to  wound him
And have Anaxarkos fall defeated

To the ground, yet instead of killing him
Or letting him go, a stronger and more
Aggressive Wesleyan made the next call
To mine lord Anaxarkos now weaker
And more enfeebled by the earlier call
From which each time, like the true
warrior did
Anaxarkos pull himself off the ground
To answer and receive fresh wounds
over
The previous battle injuries and then
Came the fourth call that saw my lord
down and
Defeated completely and unable
To get himself up, and only then did
The haughty Wesleyan leave him there
on
On the defeated ground, and drive away
Quite victorious in his unflagged chariot.
In the palace they doth comment that
thus
My good lord was treated and punished
for
Lying to the Master.

HECTOR       A punishment
Would have been to kill him, wouldn't it
have?

ELOWYN    Sergei! Where is Anaxarkos right now?

SERGEI    Very badly wounded my lady, and
          Is retreated to the camp, wherein is
          He in comforting unconsciousness lain
          From which his doctor hath him revived
          to
          Have his near fatal wounds treated that
          were
          Pronounced lucky to have spared his
          vitals
          Organs and thus in the camp he is now
          being
          Tended to.

HECTOR                    Very well. Sergei. Thank you.
          (Sergei leaves.)

HECTOR    Elowyn, but stay on and hear me speak.

ELOWYN    Speak no more to me, Hector for I have
          Nothing more to say, but allow me to
          Leave this room and retire to mine
          quarters.

HECTOR    Nay, but allow me to ask thee just one
          Time again: wilst thou end this conflict,
          now?

ELOWYN    No. I will not.

HECTOR                    Very well. Then, neither

Will I discuss with thee further what is
Too late to end now when it should have
not
Ever been begun, but instead I will
Make a fresh request and plead with ye
quite
Differently but hear.

ELOWYN                              I feel not too well.

HECTOR   My plea will not take too long, sister,
now
That this war will proceed to its fair end,
Which doth encertain a battle between
Wesleyan and Anselm, wherein of the
Two will one survive, my plea to thee is
This that should Wesleyan be the one to
Die, and should the other three stay
survived
To ascend the won throne of Axainos
By stepping across and o'er the body
Of their  brother, I do plead here with ye,
To never yield the truth to the sons of
Ortellius that they have killed not the son
Of a charioteer, but one of their blood.
Let the secret die when Wesleyan dies.

ELOWYN   Thy passion doth overrules thee, brother.
(Enter Tom)

TOM        The crowd outside doth throweth stones and does
           Beat the doors demanding to be let in .

ELOWYN     Ensure that a Guard is posted at the
           Entrance and further fortify the doors
           Whilst accompanies thou Lord Hector out the
           Back entrance to the palace whence will
           He give orders to have this crowd
           dispersed.

## Act 4 Scene 6
### Camp of the Ortellii, Battle field.

PREFECT  Bring the King here, by the lights of
torches
Whereby his wounds to be cleaned can
be seen
The better.

ANAXARKOS          Leave me. I can walk.

(Enter Dion)

DION                                        Brother.

ANAXARKOS Dion, come in here and speak thou
with me;
Pleas, leave us to speak alone, physician.

PREFECT  The cleaning of the wounds is yet not
done.

ANAXARKOS To be completed at a time hence.
Thanks.
(Exit Prefect)

DION  I see thy wounds are deep, indeed,
brother.

ANAXARKOS Sit here by me, and talk to me of that
We have both been through the man's
viciousness.
The effects of what we have both

suffered;
Whereof I wish to know thy mind and
thoughts.

DION Well, his treatment towards thee was
much worse
Than it was to me, in whose damage he
Hath less belligerence achieved and hath
Therefore I think caused less of bloody
rage
The sort in thy countenance, I perceive.

ANAXARKOS Dion, the anger that I feel now should
Have felt when aface with his sword, but
Then I felt anger not towards him but
Towards myself as though what he was
to
Me doing was my fault not his and why
My emotions were thus aligned I can
Understand not.

DION Our natures are diff'rent
Brother, art they not, for thou art the high
Philosophe and I, the paltry warrior.

ANAXARKOS Thou dost not understand my intent,
but
Tell me, of the moment that he attacked
Couldst thou unnatural intensity
Feel of his anger towards us as though

'Twas him not his friend Aristos
slighted?

DION      His agitation certainly was done
Exaggerated when he called me names
Like "son of a whore" and attacked
incensed as
Though to kill and then did not follow
through,
But then neither did I retaliate
In the manner that I usually do.

ANAXARKOS Admit it, Dion, that man hath a
power
Strange o'er us, but, you make as though
to
Return to the field, but tarry a while
And listen to my words that are to be
Told to ye: one time during the fight
when
His lance had me pinned upon the
ground did
He stand above me inflicting wounds on
Me above my sweating eyes that
happened
On his face, to look at his hate filled gaze
Through the pain and hurt of my
wounds that he

            Gaveth me I felt almost love for him.

DION        Stop it, brother.

ANAXARKOS                    No, but the narration
            Of the thing is as it was and fear of
            His power over us to feel not hate
            For him is what frightens us for it doth
            Endanger not this war but us and our
            Existence, which he will exterminate
            After he hath played with all of us to
            Then eventually condescend to kill
            Us, and before that must he be first
            killed.

DION        We will kill him, brother be thou not thus
            Affected for we will take his life in
            Return for his treatment of us; that much
            I do thee I promise right now at thy feet.

ANAXARKOS Yes, Dion, and my only happiness
            now
            Is that at this very moment Anselm
            Fights a battle with this man, for whom I
            Feel hatred now more than anything else.

DION        But…

ANAXARKOS            Hopefully Anselm inflicts
            upon
            Him ten wounds for every single wound

that
Wesleyan inflicted upon me.

DION                                        But
Anselm is not at battle at this time
With Wesleyan.

ANAXARKOS          What is is he doing then?
(Enter prefect)

PREFECT   My Lord, the chariots of Lord Anselm
And Herakles are here arrived right now.


ANAXARKOS But what? They have arrived here in
the camp?
And why are they not fighting in the
field?
(Enter Anselm)

ANSELM   Brother how glad I am to see thee well.

ANAXARKOS Anselm, what for art thou here in the
camp?

ANSELM   It was in the field that thou wast grievous
Downed and so we came to see how you
are.

ANAXARKOS Why sir, how very kind and
brotherly
Of thee, and do tell me is it also

        Silly spring outside from whence thou
        hast for
        Me plucked from the garden some
        weeny flowers
        To make my little boo-boo feel better?
        (Herakles enters.)

ANAXARKOS Herakles, as well, both of you here
        In the camp for sick room visits instead
        Of attacking the enemy at field.
        Anselm, when thou wast born did the
        Gods say
        This boy the greatest of all warriors
        Will terrorise the foe upon the field
        To them vanquish with greatest ease;
        alas,
        It cameth not to pass and doth prove that
        Even Gods are not above telling lies.

HERAKLES    Anaxarkos?

ANAXARKOS               Herakles, Stay out of
        This, and Anselm, tell me the reason why
        Thou dost disregard that one dangerous
        Man playing with us unceasingly; and
        Singly: injuring us, hurting us, and
        Humiliating us, and yet though dost
        Regard him not?

ANSELM            Brother, I was worried…

ANAXARKOS The while some third king that is
           totally
           Inconsequential to this war's progress,
           Thou dost chase and make proud vows
           to kill, and
           Those that thou needest to kill, to slay
           them
           Not once, but ten times over thou dost
           run
           Away from; if thou canst prove not thy
           worth
           By killing Wesleyan, then give thy arms
           To someone that can do the needful task.

ANSELM  What did you say? No, Herakles, I want
           To hear what he said. Repeat thy last
           words.

ANAXARKOS Repeat my words why won't I for
           what have
           I said that's wrong, and can't be repeated
           Not once but a thousand and ten times
           o'er:
           Give thy sword to one can kill Wesleyan.

HERAKLES  Sheathe thy sword, Anselm; what is
           this that thou
           Doest; are ye out of your mind, man?

ANSELM  Cut the head of any man who says to

Me, give my arms to another person.

ANAXARKOS  In the circumstance, I said naught
that's wrong.

ANSELM  Who art thou, to tell me what to do and
What not to do; who art thou the man, nay,
The warrior, that can kill the enemy
By weapons not, but by telling falsehood?

HERAKLES    Anselm. Listen to me; calm down;
control.

ANSELM  I come to ask after his wellbeing to
To get thus insulted, but who is he,
That I can recognise no more and that
Appears to be a stranger that doth thirsts
For blood, power and victory so much so
That he forgets his mode of conduct to
Speak thoughtless words, which doth show how greedy
He hath become for the throne: to fight for
Such bloody-mindedness seems not worth it.

HERAKLES    Think not the worst of thy brother,
Anselm.

ANSELM   What else should I think?

HERAKLES                                    First, sheath
            thou thy sword
            And calmly think. Perhaps, he is correct?

ANSELM   Correct about what: in his saying that
            I know not to my job properly?

ANAXARKOS Herakles, enough, but the fault was
            mine.

HERAKLES    Anaxarkos, leave this to be sorted
            Out between us two, Anselm, direct thy
            Wrath at me and speak about Wesleyan.

ANSELM   Then art thou also saying that I am
            Not fighting properly?

HERAKLES                                    What I
            say is
            That we should to thy brother's words
            give some
            Credence and think with calmness of the
            mind,
            Free of choler as to whether he doth
            Speak, to some extent, the truth that
            needs to
            Be by thee accepted, which is why are
            We avoiding Wesleyan.

ANSELM                                    Am I not

Doing the best I can in this bloody
And senseless carnage that's on outside;
no,
Herakles, with thy silence do not treat
me,
But answer my question since we all
seem
To have lost the eloquence we once did
Have, but answer thou this that I am not
Afraid of Wesleyan, if that is what
Thou thinkest of me.

HERAKLES                    But no, perhaps, not
Afraid, but maybe thou art reluctant
To fight him, and towards this have I one
Question for thee to answer: dost thou
feel
The same reluctance that you felt at the
Beginning of this war, when thou faced
the
Grim prospect of fighting thy own
grandsire,
Thy teacher and thy relations? Why is
The silent treatment now thine towards
me?
But in this silence, I doth hear the truth;
And in the truth doth lie the answer to
Thy problem, which is thou didst

             overcome
             The feeling of reluctance to kill thy
             Kinsmen, and now the same is to be done
             For Wesleyan: thou did kill Abdon; now
             Must thou in manner same kill Wesleyan.

ANSELM    But this time, it does not make any sense
             To me that my grandsire and my master
             Knew as knees that bounced me as a
             baby
             And hands that taught me right from
             wrong, but this
             Here man, Wesleyan, is and always
             Been nothing but enemy, and from
             whence
             This turncoat love I cannot understand.

HERAKLES    Most things in his world exist beyond
             our
             Cognisance, my friend and therefore try
             not
             Overthink it, but try to act it out.

ANSELM    Thou art are right for my emotions
             explained
             Are now understood and to overcome
             The easier found. Brother I do myself
             Put upon my knee to have ye forgive
             Me that was wrong, that accepts thou

wert right.

ANAXARKOS That thirsty man has a savage power
o'er
Us all that doth dry in us the sap of
Resolve to drain us and to make us feel,
And think, and behave in ashen ways
that
Us destroy and instead animate him.

ANSELM  No longer, brother, for the bloodlessness
Of my behaviour in my past hath been
Left by me now and from on my resolve
Knoweth nought but certainty and acme;
I assure thee that the next time we shall
Meet this firmament will not be
burdened
With the life of a man named Wesleyan.
(Herakles and Anselm and Dion leave.)

## Act 4 Scene 7

### House of Hector, Axainos

(Noise of the roaring mob outside)

TINA    What is it that has occurred?

TOM    The Lady Elowyn is missing and I have been sent to look for her.

TINA    Missing?

TOM    Its what he says.

TINA    I would just disobey the master's orders, if I wert thee, for unbeknownst to him, I let the prisoner out the dungeons this morning.

TOM    Thou let him out?

TINA    This morning and must he at this very moment be wherever she is somewhere wringing her neck.

TOM    Well then, my orders are to look for her and that I will do as I am told; so say nothing about the prisoner to the master, who wants to know of his sister and is ignorant yet about the other. Go thou within and pretend to search her room.
(Exit Tina. Enter Hector)

HECTOR    Butler, hast thou searched her quarters?

TOM        The maid is there, my Lord.

HECTOR     Also make enquiries whether the lady
           hath left the house.

           (Tom leaves; Tina enters)

TINA       Her room is empty and her bed is
           unslept in.

HECTOR     The other servants, have they seen her?

TINA       I did not ask. Must I?
           (Enter Tom)

TOM        I spoke just now to the wretched man,
           the beggar who sits in front of the house
           and he told me that he saw her leave the
           house early this morning and walk down
           the small dust path at the back of the
           house.

HECTOR     Was she alone?

TOM        Accompanied by Sergei the guard, said
           he.

HECTOR     That path leads to the stream and that is
           where she could be at now and I will
           there immediately.
           (Hector leaves)

TINA       My lord should know that the prisoner
           hath also escaped, but the master is

already gone before we could tell him and warn him for if he did not hear or he was not here, when I was speaking to tell him then we be not the unfaithful.

## Act 4 Scene 8

### Aristos' camp, Axainos

ARISTOS    The fight, my man, the main fight, and
the real
Fight is here and finally upon us,
Wesleyan, and now, in these final hours,
When the need is firm resolve to attack
The beast that doth stand before us in its
Last hours, dost call'st us to atrophy
These precious moments that shouldst
instead be
Spent in reflection and not in talking.

WESLEYAN    To disappoint you or to disobey,
My friend is one thing I can never do
Or intend to do, and the thing that will
Kill me in the merest thinking of it.

ARISTOS    So then, thou, waster of the precious
hour,
Pray do say for what reason do we stall?

WESLEYAN    The King of Ibrahimya needs must
drive
My chariot, and yes, though while his
haughty
Nonce was to me conveyed, I wish to
know
The reason of his stubbornness to stress

The point that if Herakles will Anselm
Drive then for certain will Hadrus drive
me.

ARISTOS His stubbornness or lack of reason is
For thee to say but 'twas that he is king ,
And thou the charioteer and to reverse
roles
Is to upset the proper order of
The world and nothing good will of it
come
And wilst I do realise that it is quite
Important to thee to impress thy class
This is not the time to teach the world of
Classlessness and egality.

WESLEYAN                                What did
Thou say to Hadrus when he did refuse?

ARISTOS But have we the leisure to discuss this:
Alright then I reminded him that doth
Herakles drive the chariot of Anselm
And we equate the status of Hadrus
With the wisdom and heights of
Herakles,
But then said he thy status is not same
As the status of Anselm, and therefore
It is below him to drive the horses
Of thy chariot; and now for the sake of

Expediency, have we not had this chat
Wesleyan, come on man, thy silence
Doth not work for us at this ev'ning
hour,
Instead tell me wilst thou bring me
victory
Or defeat; that's now entirely on ye.

WESLEYAN   Anselm will be mauled, tortured and
troubled
To his death.

ARISTOS                    Well said, my friend, and now,
take
Thy mind off of yourself for whosoe'er
You may be, you are us and will always
Remain us even when we have this war,
And throne, but tell me have you all you
need.
I won't have thee wanting against
Anselm.

WESLEYAN   Those the sons, that sit smug and
happy in
Their lives that I have bestowed upon
them,
Are objects of my hate, and hate is all
I need and that I have in plentiful.

ARISTOS   But I ask of the specifics, my man,

Weaponry, and the other comparables.

WESLEYAN   I have weapons stronger than Anselm
does;
The lightness of hand, the sharpness of
darts
Over and above that which Anselm hath;
Physical strength, courage, and
knowledge of
Weaponry, and prowess of aim above
And over Anselm's ken; and a second
Bow made by the celestial craftsman,
though
Fallible, yet superior to Anselm's.

ARISTOS   Then there is nothing more that thou
dost need?

WESLEYAN   My need is a driver who will my
wheels
Drive like Herakles that does the wheels
of
Anselm drive. My need is Ibrahimya.

ARISTOS   All right then, leave it to me and I will
Ensure that damned Hadrus drives thy
chariot,
But know thee that he maybe king, but
hath not
Skills a driver hath with his ceaseless and

Inane talk and works not as a team with
The warrior, and therefore at this time when
Thou an immense responsibility
Dost carry on thy shoulders, thou needs must
Tell me if thou art certain in thy cause.

WESLEYAN   I am certain.
(The sound of the Trumpet)

ARISTOS                          There is the call for the
Battle announced. Is there anything else.

WESLEYAN   Just this, my friend, that thou did me support
In my wayward conduct against the two,
Whom had I killed I would have ta'en us to
Strength, but know this that from now onward do
We go straight onto victory, which doth
Render my treatment of the brothers but
A preparation for the final bout
With Anselm, during which each strike that I
Did so mercilessly wield upon his
Brothers to then let go alive, will be
Doubly wielded upon Anselm whence

will
Be with each stroke not once but many
times
Over be killed for I will not let this son
Of Elowyn go alive for thee.

ARISTOS  I am pleased to hear that and now there
is
The second call; let's leave. All strength
to ye.

## Act 4 Scene 9

### By the banks of the River Hyphasis

SERGEI    It is not safe to be here, my lady.

ELOWYN  By these are calming waters awhile,
        Sergei
        And whereby need I to be removed in
        Reverie for a while, here, where this last
        Moment shall be mine alone where thou
        whilst
        Leave me for some time to reflect in
        peace.

SERGEI    My orders allow me not to leave ye.

ELOWYN  Yet I do command thee to leave, Sergei.
        (Sergei leaves. Enter Barobus )

ELOWYN  Where I quiet in the blessed solitude of
        The waters' peaceful sounds can ease the
        pain
        Of mine embattled mind, and with
        softness
        Of the wind that reflects the light as the
        Gentle riffles to aid and reassure
        My anguish unto bless'd oblivion;
        And this moment is to be mine awhile
        To forget the past that hath been opened,
        Wrenched to burn and smart with

       realisation
       That though things could have different been, a man
       Or woman hath no power more than to move
       Or be moved, be pushed or be pulled by the
       All powerful air that in concordance
       With the wiles of fate doth sometimes gently;
       Or harshly controls a powerless world;

BAROBUS Why, how nice is this picture that I see:
       The quintessence of innocence doth sits
       By the Pontus to sooth her pain and think
       Upon her misfortune that with so much
       Helplessness and so much regret did create
       An entire human being out of a mere
       Mistake: yet, a human mistake that is
       Hated upon, and hurt and laughed at by
       All, alternative to the empire
       Made out of the folly of a princess.
       What immeasurable power hath mother;
       And yet look ye world at her right now, at
       What frailty hath she, and what helplessness.

ELOWYN  Who let thee out?

BAROBUS                    They let me out, or did
          I let myself out when I killed them all
          In the house and in the manner that I
          Will thee now kill.

ELOWYN               What do you want from me?

BAROBUS I went to the battlefield and  found that
          He hath died.

ELOWYN             Who?

BAROBUS                    Thy son hath died,
          woman.
          Wesleyan is dead and nay, nay not he
          But me, I am dead and in the field have
          I breathed my last, but what noise is that,
          And there is a guard I see comes this
          way,
          And why my mother, carest thou so
          much
          For my life, but I am gone now for a
          While to be back.

SERGEI               I heard someone spoke here
          And it is not safe for you to be here.

ELOWYN  Hast thee news that Wesleyan hath been
          killed?

SERGEI     All we have is unrest in city.

ELOWYN    Hast thou heard of Wesleyan's death,
       Sergei?

SERGEI     I have heard of naught, but the noise and
       the
       Violence hath increased and I have not
       why.

ELOWYN   There is he again, guard! Behind thee!
       Look
       (Enter Barobus. Barobus kills Sergei)

BAROBUS   Anselm killed me, but say not to aught
       that
       I was down, defenseless, the ground was
       wet;
       Yes, I was defenseless when to death I
       By Anselm was put in manner same now
       With mine own, my own live hand, my
       own death
       I shall avenge by killing thee will I
       My life avenge by striking thee to death.

ELOWYN   You will kill me Wesleyan?

BAROBUS                         I am he
       And I am dead. You killed me as I will
       Thee now kill.

ELOWYN                   Is there anybody there?

BAROBUS	Thou art scared? Yes, thou art scared. I like that
To see thee scared.

ELOWYN	Somebody help me, please.

BAROBUS	But, knowest thou not at this late age of
Thy life that no one helps, and no one helped
Me when Anselm killed me, and now no one
Will help thee when I will thee kill soon now;
No one ever helps anyone, and thou
Deserves to die.

ELOWYN	Wait!

BAROBUS	How must I wait when
I am now gone where there is no more waiting
Where time is bludgeoned along with the man?
When alive, the lives of your sons was my
Gift to thee in return for that which thou
Didst to me give my life; nay not life but
Thou this unceasing humiliation,
Struggle, torture, trauma, didst give me and

Now in return for that hellish life's birth,

I, mine saintly mother mine, give thee
death.

(Enter Hector with guard. Barobus
killed.)

ELOWYN  It was the scribe, that insane scribe.

HECTOR                                    Dead now

And thou art bleeding. Let us leave for it

It is not safe. The city doth burns yet.

ELOWYN  Wesleyan hath died.

HECTOR                        Yes.

ELOWYN                              When?

HECTOR                                        At Noon.

ELOWYN                                              How?

HECTOR  It is not safe to talk right now and here.

ELOWYN  I wish to know. Was he down,
                defenseless?

## Act 5

CHORUS   Did he die? Was he down and
defenseless?
But let us go back a bit to there when
Aristos had King Hadrus to agree
To the chariot of Wesleyan ride, and
Hath dawned the final morn: ten and
seventh,
The last day the battle, to long
last
Seal the fate of Axainos and to crown
Victors and the true owners of the land.

 At start of day did Wesleyan step
Forth to the fray that began with the two
Warriors meeting in the middle of the
Field to exchange the now worthless
vows of
Valour when the air was tense and
soldiers
Both looked fraught as their men the
rules agreed
Then stepped back ready to summons of
blares.

The two men then their chariots boarded
and

Each other faced  to begin the battle
By raising their bows to pour forth
arrows,
And the still air filled with the sounds of
the
Bows strings twanging loudly, and the
deafening
Clatter of the wheels of their fast chariots
Mixed with loud thwacking hits of the
arrowed
Targets and the loud roars of the soldiers.

The first challenge did result in victory
For Wesleyan, when he first overcame
Herakles who did drive Anselm's
chariot,
And then dislodged Anselm with a
superb
Hit to enrage Dion watching from the
Sidelines, goading on his brother, telling
Him to keep his eyes upon the target;
Despite it, the second victory went
Also to Wesleyan, with third and fourth.

To the astonishment of some and the
Expectation of a few from then on,
In every challenge Wesleyan seemed to

Have the upper hand even when Anselm
Initiated attack did Wesleyan
Overcome it with sheer supremacy,
To wait for the next attack and the next
Method of Anselm, whereat Wesleyan
Had as answer not one but ten diff'rent
Retaliatory methods for though
He had not the dart of Ilmarinen,
His ordinary shafts were handled by
Him with such skill and talent that they seemed
Enough to counter extraordinary
Weapons and Anselm's military skill.

Now and then to the relief of his men
Anselm did gain a slightly upper hand,
But Wesleyan soon retrieved his control.
When Anselm dislodged Wesleyan off course,
Wesleyan soon regained direction to
Continue the battle, or when Anselm
Did succeed to pierce Wesleyan in the
Armour by a shaft, he removed it and
Continued to battle. No strategy
Of Anselm proved definitive to make
Wesleyan seem unbeatable with his
Thirst for victory, determination

To succeed and his supreme confidence.

Then why did things turn around as
they?
Was it because that amongst those
watching
If not from the sidelines from beyond the
Pale of perception was the goddess of
Fate, quite fickle minded and wild, that
did
Then decide upon a whimsy that the
Battle should favour just Anselm
wherefor
She decided to intervene in her
Friv'lous manner and change the course
of war.
Thus her thought being the command
whereat did
The sounds of Wesleyan's chariot silence
Suddenly as its wheel got fastened in
The ground to render him immovable.

When this happens in times such as these
During a war, the rules of battle state
That the driver's task it is to get down
And unfasten the wheel, while the
warrior

Continues to fend off the opponent.

Those are the rules, but this reality,
Wherein the driver of Wesleyan was
A king and not a charioteer and he
Refused to dislodge the wheel saying
that
It was way below him to jump down,
and
To kneel upon the ground, and commit
to
Such a menial task for a man of so
Common a birth by one born higher than
he.

So Wesleyan himself jumped down and
while
He pushed against the wheel to free it
from
The mud, he heard above him the sound
of
A bow being stretched, and looked up to
see that
Anselm was standing there with bow
aimed at
The neck of Wesleyan defenseless down.

"Brave" said Wesleyan a low to Anselm.
"That thou shouldst kill a man not in
combat
Fair, but when he is down and thou on
height;
When he's unprepared and thou art
weaponed."
Anselm replied, "Was not my young son
too
For battle unprepared, defenceless and
Down when thou didst despite that put
him to
His death?" With these words did
Anselm release
The pressure of his finger on the string
Of his bow, wherewith did the shaft
came at
Wesleyan with an incredible speed
To pierce him in the neck, and bring him
to
The ground instantly dead, of life devoid.
Therewith it was all over: the war of
Axainos was over. All that remained
Was to put the others to death that were
Already dead for Aristos was all
But killed when Wesleyan was put to
death.

In the city, all had fallen silent
The old regime had gone and the new would
Now arrive making the people unsure
Of their fate as they for the victors
stayed.

## Act 5 Scene 1
### House of Hector, Axainos

<blockquote>(Outside is the victory march of the Sons of Ortellius into Axainos)</blockquote>

TOM  News on streets is Lords Aristos, Norman and Leroy have all been Slaughtered and all sons and the supporters of Honorius' clan have been put to end.

TINA  It is all truly over for us.

TOM  Is she well and is she resting yet?

TINA  Hurt badly from the attack and unwell all last night, she was, but recovered slightly this morning, and is now walking with some assistance. The mistress, she hath instructed me when Lord Hector arrivedeth that I am to call her for she hath expressed a wish to speak with him.

<blockquote>(Enter Lord Hector)</blockquote>

HECTOR  Is she well?

TOM  She is my Lord and the maid is bringing the mistress in for she hath expressed a wish to speak with thee.

(Tina brings in Elowyn.)

ELOWYN  Have you met with my sons as yet,
Hector?

HECTOR  They are, sister, at this very moment
Arrived at Axainos' gates, and I must
From here to the palace proceed to greet
Them at the entrance and to welcome
them,
But thou dost look quite unwell and I
hope-

ELOWYN  Some pain, that is all, and hast thou with
thee
The information that I asked of thee?

HECTOR  I have the information, but I once
Again do implore you to let it go.

ELOWYN  I wish to know of it, and I will know
Of it now with authority, as my
Sons are newly Kings: so tell me, in
which
Place does the body of Wesleyan lie?

HECTOR  His remains hath been handed o'er to his
Family that wisheth to do last rites.

ELOWYN  We are his family, Hector, and those
That have raised him from boyhood shall
be by

Us compensated for their losses, and
Whatsoe'er might have followed his
birth, the
Pangs of his entry into this life were
Borne by us who are his parents and who
Will his buriers be, and therefore have
thou
His body brought here for us to inter.

HECTOR Does the lady realise that in wanting
This, she will release the truth of his birth
To his killers, therefore the lady should
Think this over when she is less unwell.

ELOWYN I am not ill and in no doubt about
Making confession.

HECTOR        Confession?

ELOWYN          Yes, my
Confession of my deeds to my sons and
To my maker; and while I do realise,
That it doth make no diff'rence to the
dead
Wesleyan to be given his rightful
Place that he did deserve when was alive,
It maketh a difference to me that
Hath the misfortune, nay fortune of life
And is duty bound to make good all the
Wrongs that she hath in her life

committed.

HECTOR   But in making right thy wrongs, thou commits
One more wrong: that in causing of thy sons,
Grief and perhaps, untold damage for I
Fear Anaxarkos whose mode of life was
Always governed by his values, which, now
With the exigencies of war have been
Wrenched from him like a skin leaving him to
Be exposed and eas'ly hurt, not able
To deal with truth that thou, unconcerned with
Vulnerability of thy newly
Valued son wilst reveal to him the crime
That he knowingly hath committed.

ELOWYN   That is the way I will pay for my deed.

HECTOR   But why can't you just let the past go for
A change and do what's quite contrary to
Thy demeanour; do what for the other
Person works instead of for thyself just.
The lord knoweth how many more wrongs are
Committed when a flawed person tries to

Make right the wrongs of his flawed,
selfish world.

ELOWYN  The flawed people, Hector, commit
further
Wrongs when they doth make right their
earlier deeds,
And yet even that flawed person is by
God made, and therefore despite faults I
ask
Thee, must one oneself cease to improve
in
Hope that the scale of their action doth
tip
At least a little to the side of right
And so must I … forgive me … for I have
Lost the train of thought and I feel not
well.

HECTOR  You must rest, sister.

ELOWYN                        We must our duty,
Hector, that is all I know, that we must
Do our duty for certain and so now
It is my duty to confess my son.

HECTOR  When dost thou wish to have the body of
Wesleyan presented thy waiting sons?

ELOWYN  Have it to the court presented on the

Day when Anaxarkos is crowned the king.

(Elowyn and Hector exit. Enter servants.)

TOM     He hath died. Billy is dead instead of us that are unfortunately alive to face the wrath of the new king whom we did oppose and whose mother we did enemy.

TINA     The only way for us now is to turn loyal to the new king, to confess our deeds and to ask for amnesty.

TOM     What if we are turned away by him or worst what if we are put to death?

TINA     Anaxarkos will be the king and he is the man who looks after his subjects. I had enemied not him but his mother who will never rule as queen and to Anaxarkos we will promise our unwavering allegiance.

TOM     And still his subjects we were not, but the servants Honorii.

TINA     There be a few of the servants Honorii are grouped to ask for amnesty, and to present their condition, poverty and helplessness at the new coronation will be their aim. We must also join their appeal to make our case. This is our only final chance. It is either that or death. Let us leave.

## Act 5 Scene 2

**The royal court, Axainos**

    (Enter Herakles)

HERAKLES   The victory procession went off well,
But hast thou told him of what is to
come?

HECTOR  Just after the brothers dismounted by
The font at the city square to greet the
People, I took them aside and I told them
The truth of the dead man and of what
his
Mother wanted. I thought it was the best
Time as the crowd did all about them
cheer
And to them I left the easing of the -
Their mental turbulence of hearing such -
Such news easier without solitude,
But the eldest's apathy did surprise
And for us now to demand of him he
Will arrive. Speak to him as best you can.

HERAKLES   Thou knowest best how to take him
forward.
I wilst leave him to better speak with
thee.

    (Enter Anaxarkos)

HECTOR	How art thou, Anaxarkos? Art thou
	well?

ANAXARKOS How else?

HECTOR		I expect you to take this in
	A manner stoic.

ANAXARKOS			As always I obeyed.

HECTOR	One cannot change the facts, but one can
	change
	One's reaction to the facts that are thus
	Placed firmly in the past that giveth way
	Now to the future, and the future doth
	Commands thee to act in the people's
	good.

ANAXARKOS What else does the future wants of us
	now?

HECTOR	She wants thee to bury Wesleyan and
	After she wants thee to ascend the
	throne.

	(Enter Anselm and Dion)

DION	They are bringing in the body, brother,
	For us to do what, to stare at the man
	That we killed not knowing that he was
	just
	Another one of us; and when we have

Our denied, hated, avenged and
murdered
Brother stared down his unseeing, dead
eyes,
Then, what are we to do after that: are
We to bury one she first commanded
Us to kill.

(The body of Wesleyan is brought in.)

HERAKLES                Uncoverest the cerecloth.

DION       He appeareth as though asleep and as
           Though he will get up this minute, curl
           his
           Lip with pride, utter some insulting
           word
           And draw out his sword, but instead he
           doth
           Senseless lie with wound upon his neck
           that
           We did inflict upon him.

ANSELM                               What will she
           Have us do after this; answer for her.

HECTOR  Anselm, I will bring her here and she
           must
           Answer for herself thy question, but do
           Forget thou not that she is ailing and

Hath been through her own hell and is in
need
Of your support; remember ye the sons
Of Ortellius, that the dead are dead to
Emotions and for their sakes forget not
The feelings, and respect those yet alive.

(Exit Hector)

DION        Anaxarkos, brother, are you all right?

ANSELM   If not how do you expect him to be?

(Enter Hector with Elowyn)

ELOWYN   My victorious sons, as a queen I greet
You with all the desserts that you have
earned
By fighting for the subjects to restore
Justice and bring back peace to this once
great
Then embattled land, but I also ask
Thee for allowance to be a mother
And to vanquished turn a mother's gaze,
Kneel down and indulge in show of
mother's
Grief as, forgive me, as I look upon
The face of my beloved son that hath
Himself proved worthy of his highly
birth.

I ask you to forgive me that the same
Hand I shook with thee in acknowledgement
Of thy valour and victory, I now
Use to fearfully stroke the face of one
That in dying let you live. He allowed
Me not to caress or to comfort him
When he was alive but offered me your
Lives and in doing so he let you win
And let me keep my head high as I now
Lower it in respect and in feelings
Of thankfulness to be allowed his case.

ANSELM   Are we allowed to ask of his father?

ELOWYN   A brilliant man, the identity of
Whom is totally inconsequential to
This present moment, which (please do hear my
Words, my worthy sons) this present moment
Doth make demands on us that are our
Kingdom's first family, and we unlike
Previous rulers, are servants to the throne
And in this time we must our personal
Feelings keep aside and harden our hearts

To put the problems of our people 'fore
And above our own so that they restore
To glory Axainos they knew in past.

DION     A minute mother for doth the tide of
Circumstance not retreat with firming of
Our hearts and a resolve to get down to
Business, but it doth advance to  become
A flood of unattended emotions
And issues that doth immobilise us
And therefore must thy past deeds need
be told
And thy past sins need atoned be not by
Just you but by each one of us for we
Now live, each one of us warriors, live
lives
Gifted to us by the villain whom we
Killed; for those emaciated warriors
Such as us three brothers to live the lives
Gifted in manner thus is but complete
And utter shame. Lucky is he who in
Dying escaped it and fie upon us
That are cursed to live out our gifted
lives.

ELOWYN  Dion, calm thy mind to listen for we,
Both Herakles and I, gave him the chance
To come on o'er to our side and become

One with us, which he refused and so
sealed
He his own fate; as for his gift of lives
To thee that was not my request to him,
But his own estate to me and so do
Not upon me put blame, also do not
Thyselves chastise for his pride and here
I
Ask you all to cease this game of blame
and
Not forget that we are now kings and
must
Do the best for the people of our land
For they have also suffered losses and
We are now to provide them their
desserts.

ANAXARKOS  Is this all about the land and wealth,
then?

ELOWYN  Yes, Anaxarkos, this is for the land.

ANSELM  You must have found out at some point
that he
Wesleyan was the same baby that you
Let go and when was that did this
occurred?

ELOWYN  When he fought that contest with you in
the

        Arena of Athens, I first found out.

DION       We were only boys then, and all these
Years have not thought it fit to let us
know?

ANAXARKOS But Dion, how could she have told us
for would
She have not lost the kingdom then and
who
Is this woman that I know not,
and who
Is she that exults in wealth and in power.
How much dire greed for the kingdom
hath she?

HECTOR  Here, I ask thee not to forget thyself,
Anaxarkos, maintain court decorum.

ELOWYN  Let us begin business of the kingdom:
The reason I have disclosed the truth this
Day is for Anaxarkos to bury
His brother, before we seat him upon
The throne of Axainos to be crowned the
King, but here we will leave to the future
King of Axainos to tell us which is
To be first: will he perform funeral
Rites of his brother first or ascend the
Throne first for both deeds are in the
people's

Interest and doth await thee, my son.

HECTOR    He should bury his brother first, we
think .

ANAXARKOS No, instead I will ascend the throne
first.

ELOWYN    Faced by the problems of the fortunes of
The morrow, none of us has luxury
To wallow in the personal poverty
Of the past: I am glad to hear of this
Resolve to rule and have the body of
Wesleyan to the bier moved to be soon
Buried by the near King Anaxarkos.

(The Ortellii lift the body to the bier. The
throne is prepared. The priests arrive.
Enter a crowd of Axainian citizens along
with Tom and Tina)

TOM    We wish speak to his highness, to Lord
Anaxarkos.

HECTOR    Say what you desire, and speak without
fear.

TINA    My Lord, we were loyal to Aristos before
this, but now have we nothing: no food
or possessions, no support and no future,
and so pardon us to be able to change
sides and become servant unto the new

king in return for favour and subsistence.

HECTOR   The supporters of Aritos can remain in
Axainos and need have no fear.

NANNA BETH Anaxarkos, Anaxarkos, hark ye
And hear what old woman speaks to
thee.

(Enter Nanna Beth)

NANNA BETH He died, Anaxarkos and thou did
not
Keep thy promise to me. Where is my
young
Grandson, Anaxarkos? Where is my boy
Whose life thou didst promise alive?

HECTOR   Have the woman taken to the palace
Where she will be looked after and want
for
Nothing in rule of King Anaxarkos.

NANNA BETH You killed your brother, Anaxarkos,
but
I did warn thee that thou wilst thy own
kill
And with thine own blood wilst thy
hands be stained.
Anaxarkos thou art a murderer.
Knew thou not that he was thy brother

and
Wast thou blind? Didst thou choose not
to see thine
Own kin and didst thou not lie to thyself
That he was nothing and no one to thee.
And why Anaxarkos, why didst thou
hate
Him so much that thou thirst to kill him
dead
Exceed thy brother's need to put him to
Death. Murder Anaxarkos, murderer.

(The guard takes Nanna away)

HECTOR    The time is upon us and we cannot
Delay the coronation further: when
Anaxarkos is crowned, the people will
Give praise and thanks and wish for their
long lives.
Let us with the coronation proceed.

(Anaxarkos is crowned king and the
people shout "Long live Anaxarkos"
"Long live King Anaxarkos".)

ELOWYN: Bury thy brother, King Anaxarkos.

ANAXARKOS I will first a few words to my people.

HECTOR    Rise not their passions. Respect the
living .

ANAXARKOS I am the newly crowned king that
        needs must
        Bury his brother that he killed to win
        This crown, but I shall not absolve myself
        Of my deed for I no more care about
        The rights and wrongs of actions, which
        the war
        Hath cured me of. It hath cured me of all
        My decency; and I can be no more
        Accused of being a righteous man that
        doth
        Think too much and act too little. So I
        With no more thought and no will to
        speak I
        Will instead act upon my estate on my
        Hatred that doth lie beneath this crown
        to
        My dead brother bury with that same
        hand,
        Wilst I kill myself. Yes, thou heard this
        right.
        I cannot absolve my crime. I can no
        Longer preach of right or wrong, but
        neither
        Can I continue to wear this crown that
        Hath been bought with mine own blood
        killdeth first.

And yet Axainos, rise not thy passions,
People be not afraid that I will kill
Myself and in that will leave thee
without
Protection, leadership or rule, but by
The powers vested in me, in turn, I
Pass my crown and throne to the one that
suits
Thee better in these times that knows
thee well
And that will give thee thy desserts in
way
Much better than can I that knows too
much
Gravity and need not to continue.
This the person better suited to thee:
Mother that as king consort hath almost
Ruled Axainos for the years my father
Ruled and she will serve thee well. And
so by
This hour long power vested in me I do
Abdicate the throne to have her as the
Next, Augusta of Axainos, as Queen
Elowyn Aelia the third whom thou wilst
Show love, honour and support as thou
wouldst
Have shown me. I now move on to the

more

Unhappy task of burying my brother.

(Anaxarkos buries Wesleyan)

This is the one now killed and now

buried

By me, with hands that have the stains of

his

Blood, these hands I will now take care of

by

Adding to the blood on it mine own, but,

Before I put an end to my life to

Share my brother's grave I first ask for

the

Forgiveness of my kingdom and my lord.

(Anaxarkos kills himself. Times.)